AUTHOR
ROACH, J.

CLASS
F

TITLE
Death duties and other deceptions

Death Duties
and other deceptions

Not for the first time, I have been asked to write an account of certain episodes in my life. In the past I have turned down these requests for what is now thought to be a rather old fashioned reason. To say that it hardly seems good manners to write about the people one has had the good fortune to know is to invite derision, as only bad manners mean anything now. The fact is, though, that I would have little of interest to write about had not so much of my life been spent as a guest in other people's houses and, in more than a manner of speaking, in other people's lives. I have usually had a home of my own somewhere, but it would not have been more than a very slight inconvenience to have lost the key. Forgetting the address would have been a more likely misfortune. In nineteen forty four my London flat was demolished by a flying bomb but a month went by before I learned of it, and then only by a chance remark from a stranger.

I had no money and no particular talent, and so couldn't sing for my supper or often return the favour. All the same, I did my best to repay the kindness of my various hosts and hostesses. I have a certain aptitude for taking pleasure in good things. Taking pleasure is the smart way of giving it, as every lover knows and every guest should know.

Times have changed and candour is the order of the day. These tales may now be told and I am the right man to tell them, firstly because I am the only man who knows the truth of them, and secondly because I am old and hard up and need the money. I am singing for my supper.

Verdon James
Villa d'Azou, Antibes 1992.

Death Duties

and other deceptions

Julian Roach

Ringpull

First published by Ringpull Press in 1993

Copyright Julian Roach © 1993

Ringpull Press Ltd
86A Church Street
Littleborough
OL15 8AU

A CIP catalogue record for this book
is available from the British Library
ISBN 1 898051 01 1

Typeset in 11/13 pt Ehrhardt
Filmset by Datix International Ltd, Bungay Suffolk
Printed in England by Clays Ltd, St Ives plc

05971360

Letters Patent

You probably know Steerham Park, as I believe the house is now open to the public. It used to take about an hour to get there from Piccadilly, but it's probably longer now, with motorways and so many people on the roads. Visit the house if you can. The portraits are more rewarding than they sometimes are in country houses, especially the Zoffany of Lady Caroline Buller and the two Van Dykes. The Zoffany is – or was – in the passageway between the library and the pretty blue room called Lady Mary's parlour and the Van Dykes are on the stair to the Gallery. The family trees of eighteenth century England must have been all branch and no stem, to judge by most of the portraits. Nobody looks remotely to be related either to their forefathers or anybody alive today, but everyone appears close kin to everybody else painted around seventeen fifty, the women especially. Zoffany's Lady Caroline is an exception. She is very much a descendant of the Edward Buller seen by Van Dyke. She has the sombre, regretful eyes and the distinctive set of the lips. You might think she'd been on the point of speaking but had decided ... what? To bite her tongue? Save her breath? Savour a private joke? Van Dyke has been entirely frank with the Buller nose where Zoffany may have exercised artistic discretion, but these two faces from two different centuries are, unmistakably, family. You could never go up to the gallery in the company of my friend Edward Buller without looking sideways and being a little disconcerted to see those same features bobbing up the stair beside you. He claimed he could never see the likeness.

I hadn't seen Edward for months on end; hadn't even bumped into him at parties or the theatre. He was taking his political career seriously and politics, just then, had become a very serious business. Edward was parliamentary secretary to someone whose name now escapes me, just as it seems to have escaped the historians, but who was then thought quite the coming man. There had been late sittings and great issues and votes of confidence and so on, but I wasn't keeping abreast of it all. I'd been in Deauville with Keith DuHamel aboard the extravagantly impractical yacht he was then in love with, and we'd sailed back in balmy weather, nearly becalmed most of the time.

A message had been left for me at the Squadron and I picked it up with one or two others after I'd had a good soak – a pleasure that DuHamel's yacht, though beautiful and well appointed, did not afford – and started on a long pink gin. The message said, "Come this weekend. Telephone if you can't." It came not from Edward but from Fanny, his mother.

I had to turn to the steward for help.

"Harrison, what day is it?"

"It is Saturday, Sir."

"Thank you, Harrison," I said. "Bring me the telephone."

I called Fanny Buller to make my belated apologies, and began to explain about being becalmed and the rest of it but she was not inclined to listen.

"Verdon. I'm so pleased you called. When could you be here?"

"I don't know when I could be there, Lady Buller. I'm in Cowes now; I'll get a ferry to Southampton and then it's a matter of trains. Goodness knows . . ."

"Don't do any of that, Verdon. Somebody can take you across to Chichester and we'll have a car waiting for you."

"Lady Buller, I'm not sure that there is anyone who can take me across to Chichester."

"Stay where you are."

She had hung up. Before I'd reached the end of the gin there was a voice at my shoulder. Fifteen minutes later my kit had been slung aboard a two-engined motor launch and I was struggling to keep my feet as it leapt from wave top to wave top. My helmsman was a Rear Admiral, only slightly acquainted with Lady Buller but pleased to perform this small favour for her. A chauffeur – not Lady Buller's chauffeur, but somebody else's – was waiting at the landing stage at Chichester. I dwell on these details to make it clear that Fanny Buller, charming when she wanted to be and imperious without even trying to be, was a woman who could get things done. She knew people who knew people from here to the ends of the Earth. It was clear that I was being summoned to make myself useful, but it was hard to imagine in what way. If there was anything in the world that Verdon James could do for Fanny, Lady Buller, she surely knew ten people who could do it better.

Making your way down the drive to Steerham, you might at first be driving deeper into woodland and not to a house at all, were you not allowed that famous far-off glimpse of chimneys and gable tops. This promising spectacle is lost as your way curves below a green slope often grazed by deer. You find it again, doubled by its own reflection – if the lilies are not too thick on the lake – as the drive leads you beside the waters and ushers you to the great door. Repton was responsible for some adjustments to the landscape, but not for Steerham's famous oddity, the Baron's Bridge. Like the bridge at Avignon, it fails to reach the other side. It is half a bridge thrown out across an ornamental water fashioned to resemble some ambling stretch of the Thames or Severn. The first Baron Buller began the bridge in anticipation of his elevation to an Earldom. The celebration was premature. The King went mad, patronage passed to another faction and the Baron ran out of money. There was no further advancement for man or bridge. He ordered the work stopped and declared himself more pleased with half a bridge than he would have been with a whole one. Ornamental ruins were, if anything, more fashionable than ornamental bridges.

A man was standing at the watery end of the aborted bridge as I stepped out of the car. Seeing his head turn, I raised an arm in greeting and after a moment felt a little foolish. No acknowledgement came from the bridge. No motion, no sign, no call. Admittedly, it was rather far to call, but not too far to see that the man was Edward Buller, my friend of a dozen years, and to feel that he must have seen me. I went into the house. Had I known more, of course, I would not have done. I wouldn't have taken my eyes off him.

I had not expected to be the only guest at dinner. Lady Buller and Sir Edwin came down. A place was waiting for Edward but he did not appear.

"I'm afraid he's working at his papers," said Sir Edwin. He said very little more for the length of the meal. Conversation was, famously, not among his interests. One talked with Fanny Buller. Whenever I brought Edward's name into the conversation, though, she deftly changed the subject. Clearly, whatever had to be said was not to be said in front of the servants. The Burgundy was deeply pleasing, so I fell into enjoying that and letting the time pass. The wine, if anything, was rather too good for the occasion, and Lady Buller noticed my appreciatively raised eyebrow.

"When I told Edward you were coming he gave instructions to decant a couple of bottles of that."

"It was extremely good of him."

From outside came a long and repeated blast from a motor car horn. It irritated Lady Buller but she said nothing. It was clear though, that somebody would be called upon at some time to account for the intrusion. We carried on eating in silence. It was good of Edward, but also odd. Odd, I mean, for a chap to leave his chair empty next to you, but order up a magnificent wine in this way. There was something else that should have alerted the hairs on my neck. I knew the vintage, you see. Years before on a sunny day, while lying in Port Meadow with a few friends, still an undergraduate, it had entered Edward's head to lay down wine against his wedding day.

"Have you someone in mind?" I asked him.

"Not at all. But I suppose I will marry."

"I suppose you will. Edward. Do you want me to choose a bride for you?"

"No. You can choose the wine, Verdon. What should I lay down?"

"Greater love hath no man than he shall lay down his wine for his friends. Aloxe Corton '19 would give you plenty of time to think about it. Probably forever."

He had laughed.

"Oh, I may not be able to wait that long."

It isn't often that your enjoyment of very fine wine will be marred by a butler entering with a crash. But that was how Benbow entered, his face bleached with shock but still able to command a certain gravity in his speech.

"There's been a mishap at the lake, Sir . . . My lady. Perhaps you should come as quickly as you can."

He was not dead, but he must have come very close. Had I travelled to Steerham by train, he would have been. My borrowed driver, however, had been given something to refresh him and then had set off to make his way back to Chichester.

"It was just a glimpse in the headlights, Sir, as I came round the house. Something in the water. I almost didn't think anything of it."

It was lucky that that he had thought something of it and that he was a capable sort of fellow, strong enough to plunge in and haul Edward – who had boxed at Heavyweight, remember – out of the water with some speed. He was also knowledgeable about what to do with the half-drowned and he'd done it without wasting time calling assistance. Only when he was sure Edward was breathing by his own efforts did he leave him to call for help by going back to the car and giving a long blast on the horn. I am sorry that I never knew the chauffeur's name and cannot properly acknowledge the debt we owe him. I remember that Edwin Buller gave him twenty pounds for the damage to his boots and clothes. And possibly a little extra for his discretion.

My part was to get Edward dry and warm with masses of towels. A fire was set in his room, the doctor summoned and at length Edward slept. Everyone spoke of "an accident". Edward said nothing, except that when I was rubbing him with a towel, rather in the way that masseurs do to chafe and warm the skin, he looked at me with numb exhausted eyes and said, "you shouldn't have come, Verdon. Shouldn't have come. It's all . . ." But he said no more, and submitted to the rubbing and towelling with as much resistance as if he had really drowned and not been saved at all.

I went down to the drawing room to tell the Bullers that Edward was sleeping. Fanny Buller nodded, staring into the fireplace.

"He has drafted his resignation. Did you know?"

"No."

"He won't talk about it, Verdon."

"You say he's drafted it. He hasn't submitted it?"

"He said that he had to wait for a moment when it would be . . . When it would not embarass his minister."

"I can see that this would not be the ideal time for the government. Any resignations now might easily be misunderstood. But is he out of sympathy with the party? Out of favour? It's not what I understood."

"His reasons aren't political. They are personal. And that's all he'll say. He was so dispirited. Not like him. Not like him. But I didn't think he would . . ." And she turned her face from the fire and looked at me. There was nothing imperious in her eye now: just pain and bewilderment. And love. She was such an entirely unsentimental woman that it usually wouldn't enter your head that she loved her children as much as any mother. She couldn't say the words "do away with himself".

I tried to be comforting.

"That's not necessarily . . ."

She cut me short.

"Let's not deceive ourselves. You saw him. He was not glad to have been pulled out of the water. He didn't care . . ."

It was true and I knew it. I just hadn't been sure that she did.

"Then we can talk about what's wrong. What's your own opinion, Lady Buller? Best to get your blackest cards face up."

She looked back into the fire. It was Edwin Buller who spoke.

"I don't know whether you know about my family. Every now and again one of them goes completely barmy. There isn't a word that doesn't make it sound comical, you know, Verdon. Barmy, loony, insane. It isn't very comical. It's a terrible disease. They rot in the brain. Rot from the inside."

"I'm sorry to be so frank, Sir, but I know of your Grandfather's case and your Uncle's. I understood that they had contracted a virulent infection of some kind."

"You know exactly what kind, Verdon. It was always put about that they had syphilis."

"I had understood that was the illness in question. You are telling me it wasn't?"

"It was better to let the world go on thinking that, rather than have everybody know the truth. A sorry state, wouldn't you say, when syphilis is the lesser of two evils? It is, unfortunately, something in the line, in the blood, in the family. The word they use is genetic. Why it comes out sometimes and not at other times, nobody knows."

"Does it have a name, this congenital affliction?"

"Buller's disease will do. But no, not strictly speaking. Only the symptoms have names. And one of the first – the first mental symptoms – is a marked suppression of the vital spirits. My uncle spent the last fifteen years of his life constantly under vigilance because of his suicidal tendencies."

I knew of the constant vigilance which had attended Sir Edwin's uncle. Frequent use of the strait-jacket was part of it.

"If the symptoms are showing themselves in Edward, it's very early but that's not unknown. If they are then perhaps - perhaps – he's right in wanting to . . ."

"Have you asked him whether he's aware of any symptoms? Whatever they would be."

"We have never talked about it."

I wanted to be clear, because it seemed hard to believe.

"You have never discussed the truth about this disease with Edward?"

Sir Edwin stared a long time at the border of a Persian rug.

"It's a thing we talk about in the family when the time comes. When there's any talk of marrying. We talk about it then and, well, people make up their own minds what they must do."

He walked across to the sofa and stood beside his wife. They glanced at each other without speaking, as fellow mourners might, arriving at a funeral.

Then he turned to me.

"We thought it had missed us."

Good wine leaves its flavour in your mouth a long time. I was still tasting the wine put aside for Edward's wedding.

The morning brought a cloudless sky and a colourless wintry light to Steerham; the sort of day that confirms the autumn and says that hard frosts are not so far behind. Some of the oaks were green and some had begun to turn. The smoke of cottage hearths rose in straight transparent columns of blue above their chimneys and crows sat motionless on the boughs or walked on the turf. I sat with Edward, who had taken a little to eat in his room, and looked out from his high window on a scene as tranquil and English as could be imagined.

"Do you wish you'd been left in the lake?"

He didn't answer for a long time.

"No."

"I'm glad about that."

"If only because it seems a rather timid thing to do."

"Killing yourself you mean?"

"Yes," he said after another silence.

"I don't know. Hamlet seemed to think it took rather a lot of courage."

"Hamlet's wrong. It just turns out to be more difficult than you think."

"Sir Edwin thinks . . . I'm just going to rush at this, Edward – I can't think of another way – he thinks you're afraid that you are going the way of your grandfather."

"Syphilis, you mean?" He nearly laughed. "No. I haven't got syphilis. Tell him."

I watched the pedestrian crows on the lawn for a while.

"Your father tells me that it wasn't syphilis . . ."

I prepared to explain to Edward all that Edwin Buller had told me, but Edward turned on his pillow and laughed a weary dismissive laugh.

"No, no. Well, I know all about that. Do they really think I don't?"

"Clearly you do."

"Verdon, the only inherited madness in this family is that each generation waits for the announcement of nuptials before they mention the inherited madness of the Bullers. But each generation already knows. They used to call it the Black Bile of the Bullers. And I'll tell you something else. It doesn't exist. It's a figment. You know what it is? It's exactly what they say it isn't. It's syphilis. The hereditary affliction of the Bullers is fornication, Verdon. I suppose you can say that's in the blood, if you must. My grandfather ended up in a sanatorium in Pau because he'd spent too much time in the brothels in Paris. But someone seems to have decided they'd rather believe that it's a defect in the blood. That's what's barmy."

"If I'm to ignore the possibility of hereditary madness, or syphilis, do I also ignore the possibility that you've contracted some more commonplace disease in the usual way?"

"Do you really think I'd kill myself because I'd caught a disease?"

"I was thinking of something banal like a broken heart. People do become very dejected about these things."

"Well, not in this case. I wanted to kill myself, Verdon. It really is as simple as that. I wanted to kill myself because I didn't want the bother of living the rest of my life. That's all."

His head fell back on the pillow and his eyes closed.

"Did you leave a note? It's the custom, you know."

"I left my resignation."

"Doesn't quite explain anything, Edward, does it?"

"It explains that I am disenchanted with politics and can't see a future for myself."

"It doesn't suggest that you don't see any future of any kind for yourself. Which is what you suggested last night . . ."

"Oh, Verdon. Can't you just accept that I can't see any future for myself? Not a future that I want. And the fact is, I don't have a future in politics, which is all I care about."

"Edward, you have a reason – and it must be a very forceful one – for believing that. I wish I knew what the reason is."

"Verdon, it's possible that you are being obtuse, which isn't like you. But it doesn't matter. There wouldn't be anything you could do about it."

Perhaps I was being obtuse. I could see that the effort of talking and even of eating the scrap that he'd had for breakfast had left him lethargic, so I prepared to leave him. As I touched his shoulder, he let his cheek fall onto the pillow and looked away from me at the wall.

"Perhaps it is a disease. I don't know. Maybe it becomes a disease. I'm rambling, Verdon. Ignore it. Just leave me, will you."

I walked slowly down the stair, and passed my friend, as painted by Van Dyke in doublet and piccadills, looking dark and saturnine and full of importance. I felt glad that there are no ancient portraits in my family. Neither I nor anyone else expects, or ever expected, much of Verdon James. As I turned into the hall from the bottom stair, Benbow was arranging the day's newly arrived post on a table. A mahogany knife-box with a slot cut in its sloping lid was used for the post at Steerham. Benbow opened it to remove a small clutch of letters for sending. Two or three of these I'd put there myself the night before, explaining my sudden change of plans to a number of people. We exchanged good mornings and he went off with the letters. The mahogany box had been in use for many years. As long as I had been coming to Steerham it had been there in just the same place. This, though, was the first time that I had noticed that it was, in fact, a knife box. A fact of no significance, unless it makes you realise that you are being obtuse. I climbed back up the stair and tapped on Edward's door.

He carried on looking at the wall as I said it. The immobility of his head was itself a complete answer. I said the words again, a mere statement, not a question.

"You are being blackmailed."

In a little while he'd told me a great deal. Of course, I knew so much of his story to begin with that there were things he did not have to explain. Rather than try to tell it in his words, it will be better to tell you in mine. I will be able, perhaps, to give you rather more of the picture that way. You know that Edward Buller was a handsome man. He would never have been less than handsome, but already at thirty the chiselling, as it were, of his dark features was becoming more heavy handed than ten years before. What had once been an occasional shade of melancholy in his expression had become more often a touch of the morose. At twenty, though, there was a blameless perfection about him that filled the eye. How many eyes must have been dimmed by tears to see it; tears quickly hidden, stored up and kept for a private time. Bear in mind when this was. A few years before, the nations of Europe had washed the earth in the blood of millions of young men. The human race, our part of it anyway, ached with their terrible absence. At cross roads and market squares, in college cloisters and on chapel walls you could read, freshly cut in stone or cast in bronze, the long and terrible list of their names. The swathe was broadest in proportion where it had cut through Edward's class; the subalterns and the Captains whose schooling and whose duty it was to lead, and from the front. They did not always lie in vaults with their forefathers or beneath the yews, but you could read their names and ranks in any church in any county, often on the South wall below a window brighter than the rest, the recent dedication of the bereft. They had all of them one rank, one title, one name on every stone. Beloved son. They were also brothers and cousins and friends, and would have been lovers and husbands and fathers. Each name was not one gap in the ranks but many. There were so many hearts to be pierced that I believe no one was immune to such beauty as Edward's in his youth, not young or old, not man or woman.

In some people, rich or poor, youth is a kind of splendour; in others, a kind of embarrassment. Richard St. Just d'Oliphant Butler-Boyle should have been among the splendid, if only to live up to the magnificence of his initials. If he'd had the seed of splendour in him, he'd have pretended that his stammer was an affectation that it pleased him to keep rather than abandon but when he stammered his body was racked by apology and humiliation. If he stammered for an unusually long time, it was as if all his clothes had fallen off. And yet, he was an extremely good fencer. Perhaps the mask was the important thing. Fencing is combat face to face, yet faceless; intimate but impersonal. Whatever the reason, something was released in him that was otherwise inhibited. He was quick and sure with the special quality of repose, even at speed, that only the best have. I was not much of a swordsman, always finishing somewhere near the bottom of the pool. I joined in so that others could have the pleasure of occasional victories without having to be very good. Really, my pleasure was to watch. It's a paradoxical sport, disciplined and elegant to the point of being ascetic, yet sensual in the extreme. A point scored is, after all, a breast pierced.

Edward was a good fencer, and easily had the beating of most of us, but not Butler-Boyle. Men who win at one sport do not generally like to lose at another, and boxers like Edward certainly do not. Boxers have an emotional foible, all the same: when a good boxer loses to a better, you'll see him throw his arms around his conqueror's neck. The etiquette of fencing forbids that sort of thing, but perhaps something like it happened between them.

They fenced and went in for a lot of foil practice together, meeting earlier than the rest of us at the drill hall where we fenced, and often staying later. Apart from that, for a long time they hardly mixed socially, so it surprised me when Edward mentioned that he'd invited Richard Butler-Boyle to Steerham during the long vacation. I should not have said it surprised me. It would be more honest to say that I was slightly put out. I wasn't the only one to feel a little resentment, now and then, at the way Butler-Boyle sometimes absorbed Edward's attention and admiration. We were a jolly crowd, and like all undergraduate crowds, very pleased with ourselves. Our great affectation was to believe that we knew everything about serious things but took nothing seriously. Our great business was talk and we believed our talk to be wonderfully bright and amusing. Butler-Boyle was not shaped for these sportive tricks. Apart from the fencing, he wasn't really a member of our crowd at all and it was hard to see how he could be. All the same, Edward invited him down to Steerham for a reading party in one of those endless Elysian summers in which I seem to remember growing up.

Do undergraduates still have reading-parties? Do they read at all? In those more primitive days education meant doing rather a lot of it. The reading party was a pleasant way of doing in the vacation what might have been too distracting during the term, which was a very busy time with lots of invitations and so on. The first essential was a congenial crowd and the second a large house for them to infest. Even then, the stands of large country houses were being severely thinned. People started to think it was better to sell up and spend while they were alive rather than be forced, when they were dead, to sell up and be taxed. Everyone who hadn't sold up had cousins who had and those who clung on mostly believed they would be the last, or nearly. The world, it seemed, had changed utterly and was still changing. The old were relieved or dismayed in different degrees. For the young it was a reason for throwing what Mr. Coward called a marvellous party, like first class passengers on the last crossing of one of those fabulous Atlantic liners, too costly to keep or run or ever build again, still magnificent but about to become scrap. Even reading could be turned into an agreeably elegant way of passing the time, a party.

The mornings were for reading. You could choose not to, of course, but the rule was not to disturb those who chose to. You could read wherever you chose to read. Hardly any one chose the library. The orangery was a favourite. The little temple at the end of the alley of yews was sought by the more confident sort of women. It was slightly gloomy inside and so not ideal for reading. If one wore white or cream, however, it set one off very well. It had been built, for no very good reason, as a temple of Triton, but was called the Temple of Diana, because Lady Diana Manners was supposed to have retreated there to read letters from her admirers. That summer Butler Boyle established himself in it, not for any coquettish reason, but probably because it was a place in which you could not be surprised and were unlikely to suffer casual intrusion. Anyone who wished to intrude had fifty yards to walk in your full view, so people could hardly come up and then affect to be surprised to find you there. Butler-Boyle was, as always, en garde.

In the afternoon you read or you talked. The idea was that if you talked it was about what you were reading. There would always be somebody who knew what you didn't and this was the advantage of reading in company. After a week, you would at least have said something like, "Yes, I really must read Spinoza".

A Jesuit friend once told me that the essence of the Sacrament of confession, the grace from which forgiveness sprang, lay in the Act of Contrition. This is the inward forming of a sincere, even if only momentary, desire not to sin again. It does not matter that one knows perfectly well that the wish is doomed as it is born. I feel the same is true of education: intention is the essence of the sacrament. A man who has sincerely said, "I really must read Spinoza," has made the important leap. A man who actually reads Spinoza has rather missed the point. He will certainly be wasting his time if it happens to be a nice day.

And then there was tea. Unless it rained, tea was always brought out to the lawn and was the signal for the bookworms to come out and join the talkers. There was no rule, but it would have been unthinkable to miss tea. I've grown old, but toast and honey at four o'clock will do now what it did then and what it has done for me since I was a child. It will make me feel that somewhere in the world there is safety. The rule was – I don't know who made these rules – that there should be no serious talk at tea time. Books were dropped. Gossip and teasing was taken up instead. The evening was dinner and talk, and gramophone records and silliness and seriousness in more or less equal proportions. Every day was the same, yet every day was different because it had been shaped by the day before, and always, the day before, you had learned something new; about books, about ideas, about each other, about yourself.

And one tea-time I learned about jealousy. Edward and Butler-Boyle walked onto the lawn, Edward stooping slightly and inclining his head to listen. I could not hear a word of what Butler-Boyle was saying, but I could hear and see that he was not stammering in the least. They would not give tea a miss, of course, but they walked in that slowly engrossed way that people have when they are walking nowhere in particular. When they reached the rest of us, I knew, they would break off talking and be cheerful and social. At least Edward would be cheerful. He'd ask had anyone heard the Test Match score and debate the value of putting on a spinner or start up some conversation of that sort. But watching them walk toward the little encampment of rattan table and chairs, I knew they had no particular thought of tea, or of joining the rest of us. Their only thought was to stretch out the last few moments they had to themselves.

It is strange that jealousy should be the most potent and consuming of emotions. Anyone who has felt its sudden onset knows that it is, quite simply, a strong disposition to kill. In our kind of society this is no longer a useful emotion and I wonder that we haven't evolved out of it. Sometimes I wonder at how terrible this emotion must be in the hearts of creatures for whom it is a pitiless necessity. I had some idea of it then, quite suddenly, at Steerham. I hadn't realised that I loved Edward until I felt the impulse to kill Butler-Boyle. I knew with complete certainty, though, that Edward loved him, just by their pace across the lawn.

I had, of course, never breathed a word of this terrible moment of jealousy to Edward, not until that day, twelve years later, when he lay pale and weak in his bed telling me how it came about that he was being blackmailed.

He looked at me.

"I ought to say that I had no idea, Verdon. But I can't. I knew you felt that. It's why you went back to town."

"Yes. I did, now you remind me. You didn't seem to have noticed at the time."

"Would there have been much point in saying anything? I knew why you left. I knew then, I mean. And it wasn't so much that you were jealous. It was that you didn't want to stay and give way to it."

"Oh. I really doubt I'd have killed him . . ."

"No. But you knew that you might have been spiteful. You could have been crushingly spiteful, had you wished, but you didn't wish, because you're better than that. You found a graceful excuse for leaving."

"I hope you're right. I'll pretend you are. You were head over heels weren't you, that summer?"

"I could cure his stammer, you know. It was like the laying on of hands. I could touch him and he'd be able to speak. It makes you feel that you have something special. He was a very good talker, too, you know. When the impediment was gone, he talked the way he fenced. He genuinely had a mind that shed light on things. The odd thing – I don't know that it is odd, really – was that by the next term, I couldn't make his stammer go away. That part of it didn't work any more, but we used to write. We met only very occasionally but we kept up the letters, long after that summer".

"I assume, the business in hand being what it is, that these were what you'd call love letters?"

He gave a little acknowledging shrug. "Partly."

"But enough?"

"Oh yes. It wasn't really a physical relationship, you know. Hardly at all. But we did write to each other for a while in those terms. Longing . . . aching . . . adapting freely from the Song of Songs . . . I'm sure you know the sort of thing."

"Yes, I do. Surely you could call it all an undergraduate exercise in the genre? I suppose to a large extent that's what it was. Are they really so damaging, these letters?"

He smiled and nodded.

"Enough to hang me. Put me in Reading Jail, anyway. He kept every letter I ever wrote to him over something like ten years."

I was surprised and it showed.

"Oh yes. We were in touch for that long."

"I'm amazed. I don't believe I set eyes on him after we went down from The University. Where did you hide him?"

"I didn't hide him."

"Unfortunate choice of word, old chum, forgive me. Where was he all this time?"

"He started a school. He had some very interesting, and not necessarily unsound, ideas about education. I tried to talk him out of it, of course. For one thing there was the stammer."

"Not an advantage."

"He said that's what assistant masters were for. It was for him to lay down the principles and inspire the troops; for others to carry out the orders in the trenches, or in this case, class-rooms."

"Pretty much the same thing, I always thought. Did it work out?"

"Better than you might have thought. The other trouble – after the stammer, I mean – was that your customers tend to be conservative in their tastes. There aren't many who want even tepidly radical ideas. Still, there were almost enough to keep a school going. Richard was fairly well off, anyway, so it wasn't a disaster that the thing lost money. Then came the Stock Market crash and he lost half his pupils and a lot of his own money at the same time. He couldn't subsidise the school any longer. It didn't pay and it wasn't ever going to. It broke his heart when he knew he had to stop fooling himself about it, because he genuinely loved the idea of education. He really believed, I think, that he could build the most important school in England, because it would play a part in changing England. He really did have that kind of faith in his ideas. It was a very grand ambition. Hopeless but grand. We used to discuss it in our letters over the years. After a time I tried to restore his sense of proportion, but it was no good. When you start a school in Shropshire, you more or less make up your own world. I could never get him to see the truth."

I will not have been the first to laugh, and to apologise for laughing, at the thought of Richard St. Just d'Oliphant Butler-Boyle, with his fine mind and a dreadful stammer, lost in Shropshire, nurturing an elite to change the world – the day after tomorrow.

"Oh, it was laughable," said Edward, "but peculiarly noble in its way. He wasn't out for himself and actually running a school, the real business rather than the idea, was a kind of hair shirt for him, I think."

"He closed the school down, presumably?"

"He died."

The one subject Richard Butler-Boyle, headmaster of Weston School, Shropshire, taught the boys himself was fencing. The boy was not to blame, as Richard made clear. He himself had been careless. He let himself be distracted – so many calamities on his mind, I suppose – turning to a sudden disturbance as his pupil had lunged. It would have been of no importance,except that the buttoned point had broken from the foil as it struck his hip. The unprotected blade, deflected inwards by the bone, entered the peritoneum. The wound was not deep, but it led to septicaemia. He was dead in a week.

"I remember your going down to Shropshire for a funeral. You didn't tell me it was Richard's."

"Would you have remembered him?"

"Certainly."

"With pleasure?"

"Oh . . . of course."

"Perhaps. I wasn't sure. Anyway, I went down and for one reason or another it was convenient to travel the night before and stay at the Something-or-other-Arms. And that's where I met him. Do you know, I thought the fellow was just being courteous. I thought he'd come down to the hotel to keep me company for a while, as I was on my own and knew nobody. You don't look at a man and say, 'hello. This fellow's a blackmailer'. You've no idea what a blackmailer might look like. Especially when it has not occurred to you that you might be blackmailed."

"What does a blackmailer look like?" I asked, "In this case?"

"This one looked exactly like an assistant headmaster at a failed private school. Do you know, I put up with his company because I thought he was trying to be kind. He insisted on buying me beer and he talked about the accident and about the school and what a shame it all was. He was rather gloomy about his prospects as a suddenly unemployed Latin and Geography teacher and I encouraged him to cheer up, the way one always does in a situation like that. 'Plenty of jobs for chaps like you', that sort of thing. You can imagine the conversation. I think I really did feel sorry for him. He kept saying what a beautiful man Richard was and how much he had valued my advice and support over the years. It didn't connect."

"I suppose when you go into blackmailing for the first time, you probably have to grope your way a little. I doubt if there's a good book on the subject you could turn to."

"He left me in the bar at about ten. Said he'd see me at the funeral and so on and then he asked me, actually asked me, if I'd mind if he wrote to me. It seemed odd. It was odd, but it still didn't seem odd enough to make me think very much the worse of him. I said, certainly, if he wished. Well, of course, he did write."

Dear Mr. Buller,

It was a pleasure to make your acquaintance, even in the distressing circumstance of Richard's funeral. I hope I was not too full of my own troubles during the evening we spent in the lounge bar. If the prospects seemed gloomy then, they are, unfortunately, no brighter now. These are very hard times for the private schools and as Weston has closed down halfway through the academic year the chances of finding a new post are exceedingly slim. Gabbitas Thring have so far come up with nothing that I could possibly consider. On the other hand, an opportunity has presented itself in a quite different field. I could set myself up, in a modest way, in the philatelic business, could I but raise five hundred pounds. My savings unfortunately amount to only a trifle more than two hundred and fifty, so I must raise the remainder where I can. There is no point in approaching a bank, of course.

On the strength of our very brief acquaintance, I would hardly turn in your direction, but I am emboldened by the knowledge that we have common bonds of affection for our late friend. He was a very good and close friend, in different ways, to both of us, I believe. In view of this connection I am hopeful that you will look at the investment of two hundred and fifty pounds in a favourable light.

It has fallen to me, as Deputy Head, to put the school's business in order and to sort out Richard's papers, correspondence etc. Anything that relates to you, which is a good deal, I will separate from the chaff and send on to you the moment I have the opportunity.

Yours very sincerely,

Jeremiah Seymour.

"You might not have noticed that you were being blackmailed, it is so blandly done."

"It almost escaped me. Do you know, I think if I'd written back to him and said no, I think he might not have gone on with it at all."

"It didn't stop at two hundred and fifty, I don't suppose. How much has he had from you?"

"More than a thousand. Quite a bit more. And he gets greedier."

Edward put another letter into my hand. The date was much more recent.

Dear Mr. Buller,

I must congratulate you on the upward step you have recently taken in your career, of which I read details in The Times. I entertain no doubts that you are destined, deservedly, for the highest office. Our dear and lamented friend Richard expected no less. This much was clear from the affectionate regard in which I know he always held you and I am sure that your appointment would have given him no less pleasure than it gives me.

It occurs to me that this may be an opportune moment for you to refresh your investment in philately. A thousand pounds invested now will, I'm sure, prove very worthwhile over the years to come. Once again, my heartiest congratulations and Godspeed.

Yours most sincerely . . .

"Have you paid it?"

"No."

"And is this enough to make you despair? Are you so afraid that these letters might come out?"

"Verdon, I'm afraid of the truth. And you know what the truth is? That I will pay, and go on paying. There's the despair. The more I do, the harder I work, the more I achieve, the greedier he'll get. And the more I pay him the harder it will ever be to stop paying him. I saw it all very clearly, like posts along the road stretching away. So I resigned. At least, I decided I would and I wrote the letter. I thought that would do it, you see. It was only when I read over my own letter of resignation that it came to doing away with myself. It seemed to me that everything in life, including life itself was pointless and polluted. Do you see it? Morally speaking, if that's not a ridiculous word to use, he has my life in checkmate. There was nothing wrong, nothing I can feel was wrong, in my affection for Richard, apart from a few excessively flowery letters. I wouldn't write letters like that today, not to anybody, but that's on the grounds of literary taste rather than anything else. Grieving is a special kind of love, isn't it? It ought to be an especially pure kind of love. And instead, it turned into this. I could see no way to go on that meant anything to me. I'm not sure I do now."

I took him by the hand. There was a long silence between us.

"Is there a way?" he said, finally.

"Of course," I said. "There always is. It's up to us to find it."

"Verdon, if there was a way out of blackmail I should think everyone would know of it and that would be an end of blackmail. But while the law is what it is, and emotions are what they are, there will be blackmail. Don't offer me any false comfort. Be a good friend and don't do that."

I found it hard to deny Edward's point. If there were an easy way to slip the bonds of blackmail, plenty of people would know of it. In those days of rather queer legislation, plenty of people were being blackmailed, after all. It seems odd, looking back on it, that in those days people were less inquisitive, less censorious and more accomodating about the sexual foibles of public figures. What they got up to between the sheets was not considered so very important as long as the relations enjoyed were enjoyed by at least one member of each sex. The black-mailer's rich seam lay in this one oddity: to sleep with your friend's wife was commonplace and unimportant; to sleep with your friend was a crime of terrible consequence attracting a jail sentence, public abomination and disgrace. The hypocrisy which is now delivered broadside was then concentrated upon a very small target, with correspondingly terrible effect. What do blackmailers go in for now? What trifles do the Jeremiah Seymours of the world snaffle up and turn to account? Nowadays of course, they work for newspapers, draw a regular salary and are far too proud to put their silence up for sale.

I advised Edward to pay Seymour but to pay the man less than he asked.

"You are not in such a weak position as all that, you know. He has a gun to your head but he can only shoot it once. He can't shoot you a little bit. If you don't pay him he has the spiteful satisfaction of discharging the one shot he's got. As long as you pay him something, he has the hope of more and he won't want to spend that one round. Write to him pleasantly and say that you can't justify quite that sort of investment in philately. Send him another two-fifty. It won't satisfy him, but it will be too good to resist, I'm sure. He'll want to stay in the game. Make a point of referring to it as an investment, the way he does."

"Why do you say that? I've always just put money in an envelope. I don't feel like writing to him."

"No. Send a cheque. Write a covering letter. Begin it 'My dear Seymour . . .' and refer to your interest in philately. You don't have to be too chummy . . ."

"I'm glad about that . . . but why should I?"

"This man probably has no relationship in the world that is quite as close, and none, I daresay, as precious to him, as this one with you. Enter into his little conceit of the investment and so on. It is a fancy of his. It tells us something important about him, that he goes about it this way. I just don't know yet why it's important. A different man would take pleasure in crudely threatening. Mr. Seymour does not. He takes pleasure – I think that is obvious – in this rather gentlemanly charade. Now when one man holds another by a chain, the chain may be pulled two ways. We can pull only weakly, but if we learn to manoeuvre him a little at first, we may learn how to handle him in the end. Already we know something of the way he inclines. So we will nudge him in the direction he already leans. When you consider it, you are more powerful than you think. The relationship between blackmailer and blackmailed is one of peculiar intimacy and there is always power in intimacy. It is a matter of waiting out the game until you recognise your power and see the opportunity to use it."

The whole family of Bullers was in a better frame of mind when I left Steerham than they had been when I'd arrived. All the same, I felt slightly fraudulent. True, I had bucked them up a little and conveyed a certain optimism. In truth, though, it was hard to see very good grounds for that optimism. I was in the same position as the rest of the world: I knew no way out of blackmail. The following week I was due to spend at Lord Beckinsale's place in Yorkshire, and it was necessary to spend a day or two in London first to equip myself for country pursuits. It seemed a good idea to find a little extra time to make the acquaintance of Mr. Seymour, the first blackmailer in my circle. The philately business was, it seemed, not just a fiction. Seymour had indeed set himself up in that line at an address in Holloway. At Paddington I went to the newsagent and made an enquiry. There were two journals on their shelves devoted to the interests of the stamp collecting fancy. By the time I'd read them through, I had learned a little about the enthusiasm and picked up something of its jargon, but the essential lure of the pastime continued to escape me. Mr. Seymour had a small advertisement in both journals, in a column of similar advertisments in the back pages. His advertisment carried a line in italics. It said, 'personal callers welcome'.

A bell rang as you entered Mr. Seymour's shop. It continued to dance on its spring for some time after you had entered and closed the door. It made rather a merry sort of noise, very much at odds with the native gloom and silence of the place. After a while the tintinnabulation ceased but the bell continued to fidget silently on its spring, as if it shared your embarassment. There was something of a wait before Mr. Seymour came into the shop from the sombre passageway that led to the rear quarters. He'd a well scrubbed sort of face and thin, sandy, receding hair that exposed a great deal of pink scalp. All in all, his head was a shining globe that greatly alleviated the gloom. He was carrying a napkin and wiping his lips and it was clear that I had interrupted him at a meal, but his manner was courteous.

"Good afternoon. What can I do for you?"

"I don't yet know enough to answer you," I said, "but I'm attracted to the idea of starting a stamp collection. Where do I begin?"

"You've begun very well," he answered. "You've begun here, and that could hardly be improved on."

"I saw your advertisment in The Philatelist."

"What gave you the idea of starting a collection? I ask because there are lots of different reasons people have for collecting stamps, you know. Some people take an interest in history and some in geography and some just like them the way other people like pictures – they are little pictures, after all, aren't they – and other people like . . . oh all sorts of other things. If I had an idea of what attracts you, then I'm sure we could start off along the right sort of lines."

I had browsed the entry under Philately in the encyclopaedia at Steerham. It had not, unfortunately, excited my interest and I had become sleepy and inattentive after a page or so. The entry, which was astonishingly long, had been divided into many sections. There were pages on the history of posts and postage stamps, on manufacture, on aspects of collecting and philatelic scholarship. My eyes had become heavy after the first few paragraphs of section one: history of the posts.

"It's the history of the thing more than anything else," I said. His eyes glowed in his already glowing face.

"Do you know, I really do think, it's a personal thing of course, but I do think that is the best basis of all for an interest in philately."

"And Geography, too, I suppose." I said. "Can't avoid it, really. Wasn't Brazil the second country to adopt the postage stamp?"

"Indeed, indeed," he enthused.

"Not that I know very much about all that, but I think I'd care to build a collection that tells the story, if you see what I mean. Rather than just an assembly of stamps."

Seymour was now beaming. Partly, no doubt, because his own interests lay in this direction – he was after all a former teacher of Geography and Latin – but more likely because an historical collection of stamps will involve rather more of an outlay of cash. He immediately probed to discover how sound the prospect of free spending might be, like a man biting a coin that might be gold, or might not.

"You realise, of course, that a collection of a definitive historical nature would not be the cheapest sort of collection to acquire – though a surprising amount can be done without too daunting an expenditure."

"Oh, I'm not especially rich," I said in the perfectly sincere way that especially rich people have when they use the same words, "but if I'm going to start a collection, I'd like it to be worth something. I shouldn't mind if it proved to be a bit of an investment, either."

"That is perfectly possible. Perfectly possible, Mr. Er . . ."

We introduced ourselves. And then with great patience, and some pleasure, at least on his part, Mr. Seymour initiated me into the first rites of stamp collecting. In the course of our talk he let me know, with some gravity, that he had a number of titled clients and that the King himself was a devoted philatelist. I allowed myself to be impressed by this fact, which seemed to me bizarre. I had a mental picture of His Majesty sitting at his albums, by a shaded lamp, inspecting row upon row of small pictures of his own profile. There were, as Mr. Seymour said, many reasons for collecting stamps. By the time I left him, I had made a number of purchases including several books on the subject and a handsome album bound in morocco leather, together with a number of stamps and covers which were to form the nucleus of my collection. I had also formed a good picture of the man I had come to think of as a sort of opponent.

While I was making the beginnings of a stamp collection, Edward recovered his common sense. I had torn up his letter of resignation and he did not draft another. Within a month or two, his friends had the satisfaction of reading reports of his performance in the House on occasions when he had to stand in for a Minister. Inner circles had always thought him marked for the top. The commentators of the press were beginning to make the opinion public property. A leading article in one of the more sonorous newspapers struck the note.

'Edward Buller is still a young man. In a man of ability, it is hard to see how this can be a very great disadvantage, and Mr. Buller is, unquestionably, a man of ability. There is in the present cabinet a number of Ministers of whom it might be said, as it was said of Lord North, that they 'fill a chair'. They have served long and have shown skill in not rocking the boat, but it is perhaps time that some of them got up and emptied their chairs. If it is still thought to be too soon for cabinet posts to be found for Mr. Buller and his like – for there are others – then at the very least, the way should be prepared for them, and that way should not be too long or winding.'

The weekend it was published, this leader caused some lively and cheerful discussion at the Hampshire House of Sir Kenneth Charteris. I happened to be staying there and Edward drove over from Steerham, having been put down to bat at five for Sir Kenneth's XI in the match played every year by long custom against the village team. It should be admitted that the writer of the leading article was a useful left arm slow-bowler batting at nine in the same team. It might also be said that the Bullers had a family connection through cousins with the proprietor of the newspaper. That is how things were done in those days and if they are done differently nowadays, I should be very surprised.

The leading article was not, for me, quite the most interesting development in Edward's career to come to light that weekend. We made our way from the house and along the lane to the pitch, debating the unpromising look of the weather. The path led us through the Churchyard where Charterisses long since bowled out lay peacefully in what Keith DuHamel once, walking the same path with me, called "that other Wisden". You know how it is with a good remark. One likes to revive it from time to time, especially, for some reason, with people who already know it. I turned to find Edward. He was some way behind, walking with Hugo Tyrwhitt's sister Marina. They were walking in that slowly engrossed way that people have when they are walking nowhere in particular. He was stooping slightly and inclining his head to listen. From time to time he swung the bat he carried, or tapped it against his toe as they paused as if it were a stick that he might at another moment toss away to the brambles without a thought. He was the only cricketer on that walk who had paid no attention to the sky. It made me wonderfully happy to see it.

I was twelfth man and was to be called on only to take on the drinks unless the batting went as low as eight, in which case I'd do the running for Tommy Whitworth who had a false foot but was the best fielder at silly point you'd ever hope to see. In fact, I was not called on at all, as the skies turned to ink and the day was lost to steady rain. The weather gave me the opportunity to exchange a few words with our opening bat as he took off the pads. His name, without omission of any part of the title that adorned it, had been mentioned to me with some reverence by Mr. Seymour. Our opener was a philatelist whose collection stood in the first rank. I mentioned that I had taken up the fancy and, as true enthusiasts do, he opened his heart to me. His warm words of advice and warnings of pitfall and snare would have been invaluable to anybody seriously beginning a collection. He thought Seymour was 'less of a charlatan' than many a dealer.

On my next visit to Mr. Seymour I mentioned the judgement of my fellow guest, adding a little embroidery to the hem of the thing to turn it into rather more of a compliment. I always hope that I am not a snob. I don't mind being thought a snob, but I wouldn't like to be thought muddle-headed. Snobbery is the error of finding things good or bad for reasons that have nothing to do with morals, which seems to me rather muddle-headed thinking. All the same, being English after all, I have lapses. It is the congenital affliction of the English, high or low. And worst of all, in-between. Seymour was very in-between. The effect on him of this aristocratic notice was a spectacle worth watching. We usually talk about people swelling with pride. Seymour almost shrivelled with pleasure and obsequiousness. He wrapped himself around the compliment like the late grape that wrinkles on the vine to concentrate its sugars. In the case of grapes, I think they call it the Noble Rot. Mr. Seymour was a snob.

I looked about his shop. It had been attended to diligently with wax polish, and his wares were arranged neatly and without imagination in bright glass cases. All the same, the room was a dingy one in a dingy building in a dispiriting street.

"Do you never think of moving to more convenient premises?" I asked him. "You are rather out of the way here."

"If I could," he answered, "I'd move to the Burlington Arcade or somewhere of the kind tomorrow. If I could."

"That would certainly be more convenient. Surely the increase in business would make it worth your while? Chaps like me would certainly be able to call much more often."

He talked of the difficulty, the cost, the risk, and he talked with undisguised longing. I took what opportunity I could to excite his imagination with the lustre of a Mayfair address without appearing to take too close an interest in his affairs.

The next letter was not long in coming.

"He wants two hundred and seventy five, Verdon."

"I think I know what he wants it for, Edward. He has ambitions to move his business to the West End. Perhaps he's found a lease. I have to say that I have been encouraging him rather."

"Verdon, why?"

"I think it's what we want."

He got up out of his chair and paced the length of the fireside rug two or three times.

"He wants enough when he's a little nobody in Holloway, Verdon. What's he going to want when he's strolling down Piccadilly? What are you up to?"

"Edward, I want him to make a success of this business of his and so should you. The difference between a blackmailer and his victim is that the victim has a reputation and a future to lose, the blackmailer nothing of the kind. The most dangerous blackmailer is the nobody. I want Mr. Seymour to feel that he is somebody. Might I make a suggestion? It would enormously increase Mr. Seymour's standing in the world if he were to be invited to write, oh, a hundred or so words a month in a respectable newspaper. Philatelist's corner. You know the sort of thing I mean."

Edward looked at me with extreme disapproval. I persisted.

"He would begin to think he really was somebody, then."

"I wish I could really follow your thought processes, Verdon."

"It would be a good thing, Edward. Mr. Seymour would be a thoroughly sound choice as a philatelic correspondent. He'd give excellent value, I'm sure."

The English class system could not be kept up by the simple self-interest of the people at the top. It depends even more on the voluntary subscriptions of those who come lower down. Seymour was clearly a willing subscriber somewhere not very high up in the marvellous arch. When he moved his shop to the West End he moved, and not only in his own eyes I'm sure, higher by a good bound. It was not in one of the fashionable arcades but Piccadilly was not too many steps away. He had brought some of his glass cabinets with him from Holloway. There they had looked finer than their circumstances. Now they looked like shabby interlopers, but Mr. Seymour stood among them, glowingly pink, his fleshy neck pinched by a cruelly starched collar, and with the air of a man who had begun to be somebody. One morning, shortly after he had opened for business at his new address I was walking down Curzon Street and saw him stop opposite Trumpers. After a moment, he walked on but then turned abruptly and crossed the street. The next time I saw him, his thinning hair was freshly cut and gleaming. It is not that he had entirely acquired the confident demeanour of other men who called from time to time at Trumpers on their way to and from their clubs but he approached as close as was likely for a failed schoolmaster. I called at his premises later in the week. To my surprise, Mr. Seymour offered me a glass of sherry.

"To be honest, Mr. Verdon, I should be glad of your advice."

"It's not usually worth very much," I said, "but I'll certainly take a glass of sherry for it."

He poured two glasses of Amontillado and leaned back against one of his cabinets as if composing a sentence whose precise phraseology carried some legal or perhaps philosophical import. He pursed his lips once or twice as if about to begin but regressed to the phase of inward gestation with a sip or two of sherry. Finally he pulled at the bottom of his waistcoat and began.

"I am considering writing what I believe they call a column in one of the more serious papers. I have been asked to do so, anyway." He managed to convey that the request might almost constitute a nuisance.

"To write about stamps, you mean?" I was impressed.

"On the subject of philately, of course." He smiled self-deprecatingly, "I would not venture my opinion on any other subject, but this is the one area in which I know whereof I speak. So to speak. You might read such a column, I take it?"

"I daresay I would. Especially if it were informative."

"Now that is just the point. What sort of information does the general reader want? I should be very glad to hear your views. They would be most helpful to me."

I gave him my views. He wished to refill my glass, but unfortunately I was late for an engagement. It seems my views were most helpful to him. I was flattered that he accepted my suggestion for his pseudonym. The little monthly corner by 'Denarius' became required reading among stamp collectors.

Edward and I were walking in St. James after lunching at his club. The moment he told me his news, I knew that he had raised the curtain on what I thought of as Act three of the drama. I hoped that there were to be only three Acts and that in the end, the play would not turn out to be a tragedy.

His first item of news was hardly unexpected. He had been called to the Prime Minister's office and was to be made junior minister, though I forget for what.

His second item had not been quite so long expected. Marina Tyrwhitt had accepted his proposal of marriage and their engagment was shortly to be announced. You will have guessed that I had encouraged the friendship between Edward and Marina and was delighted to hear what he said. She was a woman of wit and a forceful character and exactly what Edward needed in a wife. Fortunately, she had decided this herself and before long Edward had had little choice but to propose to her.

He stopped and leaned against the balustrade of the bridge.

"I'm not sure I know what I'm doing, Verdon. I find that I've promised to marry Marina. How can I do it? She is so marvellous and she makes me feel so extraordinarily strong that I lose sight of things. But I can't . . . I can't marry her."

"Why not? She is exactly right for you. You know it. She has judgement, Edward, and nothing could possibly overawe her. Exactly the woman for Downing St."

"Verdon. I wasn't putting her forward for a professional vacancy. I asked her to marry me because I love her."

"I know that, Edward. It's just not the sort of thing a chap mentions, except when he's in love. Which I'm not. Which is lucky for you because if I were it would be with Marina."

"But I can't marry her."

"You must."

"But you know why I can't. I can take the job. The worst that can happen is I'll have to resign, and I'll have no future. Well, nowadays I can look on it with a certain amount of equanimity. I'll take what comes. But I've no right to let . . . to take Marina on board to suffer, if it comes to it, exactly the same fate. It's obvious, Verdon. One can't do that and I shouldn't have put myself or her in this position. I did, because . . ." He peered over into the water for a long time. It wasn't a sentence he had to finish. Not to someone who knew Marina.

"Edward, Marina's happiness is important to me, too. As is yours. I think it's very important, not just for the two of you, but for lots of people. For the country, even, if that doesn't sound too silly. We have to sort this business out for good."

He looked at me and shrugged wearily.

"But we can't."

"I will. I think I can do it, it will cost quite a lot of money, but I think it may be settled once and for all."

There was a slight alarm that he was anxious to turn to amusement on his face as he turned to me.

"Whatever you're suggesting, I hope it is entirely legal, Verdon."

"Legal as Letters Patent, old chum. It occurs to me that you should settle a date for the wedding somewhat after the King's Birthday, Edward."

He looked at me with a sort of amused resignation.

"If you say so, Verdon."

"Let's go to Bond Street and I'll help you choose something for Marina. You cannot entirely trust your own taste in these things."

Lady Buller fingered the single row of pearls and let them fall back upon her bosom. I always want to touch perfect pearls but contented myself with enjoying their soft glow while waiting for her to turn over what I had said. At length she spoke, ticking off her points on the fingers of her left hand.

"There are three things, aren't there? How it is done? The

practical side, I mean; to whom does one go these days?.. Then there's the money. What will it cost? How much would be sensible? And then there's the problem of . . . overcoming one's revulsion."

She turned in her chair and looked at me. The turning of the light on the orient of the pearls was lovely to see. The lucidity of her mind was no less pleasing. I was glad not to be dealing with her husband, who would, I knew, have been far too much prey to his emotions. The revulsion was the problem. We were discussing certain aspects of the English appetite for class distinction. The English are no longer entirely agreed that their class system is a good thing but at least it has a kind of honesty. Nobody pretends that it isn't there, or that it is anything other than what it is. Where there is an attempt to deny, however unconvincingly, that the game is going on at all, it is difficult to arrange an honest market in tickets to the ground. As long as you have the right money, there is no difficulty about buying yourself a title in England. Once upon a time, you gave the cash directly to the King, who was glad of it because he was always hard up. Nowadays you hand it to the Political parties because they are hard up. When I was young there were very many men who had answered their country's call in the Great War – the call for bully-beef, say, or green paint – and by their patriotism amassed huge fortunes. The Prime Minister's party was badly short of money and the trade in honours became so brisk that for a moment or two it was regarded with distaste. The indignation was perhaps strongest in those who had come early and paid dear for honours that were later sold cheap because so many chaps like themselves had already got them. Parliament passed an Act to abolish the trade. They might as well have passed an Act to abolish the North Pole, but it at least had the effect of restoring the air of hush and circumspection proper to a dignified business.

"I understand that fully, Lady Buller. Your revulsion is quite natural and I share it. But in the present case, I look at it like this: while we're sitting here, someone not very far away is necking a chicken for our soup. Mrs. Parry is in her kitchen dressing a hare. There's a natural revulsion to be overcome in doing these things but it is worth it for the excellence of the result. I'm sure we will find the same sort of thing in this case. We are going to take someone who makes your nostrils wrinkle and turn him into something altogether more acceptable and much less noxious."

"One might feel badly about the other people on the list, all the same."

"There'll be quite a lot of third rate politicians and doubtful bankers in the list. A blackmailer will surely find people to feel at home with."

"I don't always appreciate your humour, Verdon. Think of all those Ambassadors and diplomats. All waiting for their K. Men of the best sort."

"There can be few subjects in which senior diplomats are better versed than blackmail, Lady Buller."

"Yes, but they don't do it on their own account. They do it for their country."

"For their country. And for their K."

"You might have done frightfully well in the Foreign Service, Verdon. Did you never think of it?"

"No, Lady Buller."

"Why not?"

"I shouldn't have known anybody. I wasn't at Eton."

"And there's your humour, of course. You would probably have ended up in Ulan Bator. Let's talk about the money. How much would one have to think of?"

"Perhaps as much as ten thousand pounds, perhaps as little as five."

I admit I was quoting these figures speculatively. It was then quite a long time since I had, as it were, been on the floor of the Exchange. She was silent for a few moments. He face betrayed no emotion. The pearls continued to glow contentedly on her bosom.

"I see. I'm glad that our honours are still worth something,

then. And the other thing? With whom does one do business?"
And then she shook her hand, dropping the pearls again. "I
suppose I do not need to know."

A few years before, if you'd wanted to be a Baron, he might
have come to you. It's not hard to spot a man with plenty of
money who wants to rise in the world, especially if it's your
business to help him on his way for a modest commission. Men
who were eager to be advanced might have heard, because
they'd made enquiries, that the place to go was the Ambassador
Club. Once your face had been seen there a few times it was
easy to strike up an acquaintance with the right man. The right
man was Maundy Gregory. Among other things he owned the
Ambassador Club, or appeared to, and had a large circle of
acquaintance, or rather several large concentric circles. He also
kept an office near Whitehall, and had you met him there you
might have been persuaded that he was a Government Officer
of a rather glamorous and very confidential kind. In his way, of
course, he was. Some thought it was odd that a man who knew
so many rich and titled people should, in the end, run out of
friends. I don't think it was odd. The man who can arrange for
you to become a lord is your friend, but once you are a lord,
you don't care to be seen with him much. He is hardly an
acquaintance. When he arranges for your neighbour to become
a lord, he is your enemy. It would not have been convenient to
disgrace Maundy Gregory, but in the end he had to live abroad,
his mouth stopped with gold. I had known him only slightly.
When he left, I was in the party of people who saw him onto
the boat train. It is not necessary to explain how this came
about, other than to say that because I was one of the few
people left in London not compromised by association with
Gregory, I was entrusted with a small role in the financial
arrangements that were to keep him in France. It is more to the
point of this tale that I knew what had become of the bits and
pieces of his business. I had, as it were, a few pages from
Gregory's address book and so knew where to go next.

The view from the window was not grand, though it offered a glimpse of the Victoria Tower down a cleft between the unimposing rearquarters of other buildings with even worse views. To make up for it, the office itself was charming. Only the filing cabinet made any suggestion of being businesslike. The carpet was a supple and delicate Tabriz and in place of a desk was a round table, exquisitely inlaid, on which books and papers lay in neat, overlapping piles, as if divided into suits. Over the mantel, where one might have expected a portrait, or an impressionist landscape, was a Tibetan prayer banner in a plain frame. Apart from these things the room was almost ascetic. The man sitting at the table was apologetic.

"I'm sorry I can't offer you tea, but I really can't bear the mess. If it came up in a tin mug, one wouldn't mind so much, but it seems to involve more vessels and machinery than the Spithead Review and I really can't bear to see it all over the place. You don't mind?"

I remembered that he had been famous at Cambridge for excluding almost every kind of food and drink from his rooms. It was remarked that he had no objection to joining other men in their rooms to wield a toasting fork. He simply did not allow it in his own. He had been known for other things, too. Brief intense friendships, brief intense poetry published in a review, edited by himself, whose life in print was brief but intense. His views, as expressed in some of his verse and a great deal of entertaining, conversation, amounted to a conviction that the remainder of history was going to be brief but intense. At least, it would be intense for those with the intelligence to realise that it was going to be brief. He was an intellectual and aesthetic equivalent of the sandwich-board man who claims the end of the world is nigh. Unlike the sandwich-board man, he did not disguise the fact that he was delighted by the idea. Alastair McLaren had become more sober in appearance and his hair was vanishing prematurely, but it was clear that he had not, like so many men, changed out of recognition between twenty and thirty. We passed the usual pleasantries back and forth, invoking the names of mutual acquaintances and other items of common recall and then glided into business. I explained all the details of Edward's case and laid my plan, such as it was, fully before him, only keeping back Edward's name or anything that might have suggested it. McLaren steepled his fingers under his chin and absorbed all of it with the impassivity of a cat in a window. Then he looked at me with an intense sparkle in his eye.

"It is elegant. I am drawn to the idea. Yes, we must put this into effect."

"I am pleased you approve."

"Once you've drawn the outlines of the thing, Verdon, it's rather like being given a pretty clock. One couldn't do other than wind it up and wait for it to strike. I should think, in principle, from what you say, any degree of distinction, however small, will do it. There probably isn't an order of distinction low enough to miss the mark."

"I'm sure you're right, but one feels . . ."

"I know what you're going to say," said McLaren. "The nature of the drama demands worthier props than, say, a British Empire Medal."

"I think so. While it would be interesting to discover how small a gong a man like this will sell his soul for, that isn't the object of this exercise. The object is to free one's friend, not to conduct an experiment."

McLaren stretched himself a little. The resemblance to a cat in a window was sometimes extraordinary.

"A kingdom would be ideal. There are usually countries in the Balkans looking for a monarch but I don't know who you'd see about that."

"I had thought of a CBE, perhaps. What sort of money would that take?"

"I've no idea. Does anyone make a market in them? People with the money to buy dignities want more than that, don't they? They want something they will hear on people's lips every day. They don't want to have to peer at envelopes, and suffer pangs if it's not there. Not how vanity works at all."

"But I suppose it could be arranged . . . A CBE, I mean. The CBE shop must be open."

"No. I won't do it. People who get those things may be quite decent, diligent souls, who have done sterling things in their way. I feel they shouldn't have to rub shoulders with a black-mailer."

"Yes, I understand your feelings . . ."

"A knighthood then? Services to philately."

"That would be most appropriate. The King will very likely approve."

He raised his slightly feline eyebrow.

"Oh? Do you think?"

"Oh, yes. He collects stamps."

"Really. What a wonderful thing to know. So beautifully symmetrical. I must take a look at your stamp dealer and then we should find a day when we can have lunch."

I suggested my club. He dismissed the notion with a glance. "Oh no. Dingy hole. Not at any of mine, either. Let's go somewhere jazzy."

This was heartening. Alastair McLaren was a member of a surprising number of clubs, all of them grander by far than mine. This was necessary in his line of work which might have been described as political arbitrage. If we were to lunch at one of his clubs, then my business would have been only one of the things on his mind. If we went somewhere to enjoy ourselves, it meant that my scheme had caught his fancy.

As it turned out, neither of us had to play the host, as we bumped into each other a few weeks later as fellow guests down in Buckinghamshire. I had been invited, as usual, because otherwise they would have been thirteen. Alastair had been invited because, I suppose, the business of the weekend could not have gone ahead without him.

By the middle of the afternoon, most of the party had taken to the river in small boats with the idea of pic-nicking on an island. If you've done this sort of thing, you'll know that while the platonic idea of the thing is very fine, the experience in the real world is usually vexatious. I stayed behind to enjoy the afternoon dozing over the view of the gardens from the high terrace of the house, which seemed a more agreeable pastime than getting wet elbows. Alastair was of the same mind.

"We shall be the dry-bobs this afternoon," he said.

We settled ourselves on a pair of armchairs and a bottle of Hock was made to apear. The earlier conversation had been exclusively political, as you might expect. It led me to wonder aloud to Alastair why, with his advantages, he remained a staff officer rather than a commander in the line. Why did he not stand for Parliament?

"No, no, Verdon. While I think I'm a very appealing sort of person, of course, I'm not everybody's cup of tea. Every so often, a politician has to make himself appealing to as many people as possible, most of them rather ugly and unimportant. Whatever that takes, I don't have it. Some people have it without trying, of course. Edward Buller, for instance."

I sipped a little of the Hock, not knowing whether this was a guess, a probe or a coincidence.

"I saw Buller the other day in Sanctuary Yard talking to a crowd of men from Liverpool. Unemployed. Probably communists. Unwashed, incomprehensible. It's not their anger that's incomprehensible, of course, merely what they say. One understands their anger perfectly. They ought to have been in London to burn down Parliament. But they weren't. They were talking to Buller, and Buller was talking to them, on terms of perfect amicability. You could see it in their faces: they thought him a very fine chap. I don't believe he understands their lives any better than I – indeed, not nearly as well as I – but these same Liverpudlians would probably have been ready to tear a chap like me limb from limb."

"You'd put money on Buller, then? In the Glittering Prize Stakes, I mean?"

"Oh, dear, I'm not a betting man, Verdon. I would never bet on a race unless I was absolutely sure that I had rigged it from start to finish, from the stable lads to the Jockey Club. The whole object of my life is to take doubtful things and turn them into certainties. But I like Buller, if that's what you mean. I shouldn't mind seeing him do well. You two were at Oxford together, weren't you?"

"Yes, but he got a first."

"Didn't get his fellowship at All Souls, though."

I realised that McLaren had not brought Edward into the conversation because he had begun to nose out his involvement in our business. It was simply the ordinary jealous watchfulness that very clever men maintain towards each other. However, to be quite safe I wanted to take the conversation away from Edward and the surest way to do that was to turn it to Alastair himself.

"But why does it satisfy a man like you Alastair? You are very much cleverer than the people you serve."

"Did you never build a sand castle, Verdon?"

I had to confess that I never had.

"Then perhaps you don't realise that the whole point of building a sandcastle is the returning of the tide, Verdon. The tide. That's the most thrilling part. You know for the first time, and never more clearly, that you may be tiny but you work in a realm of enormous forces. The more elaborate the sandcastle, the more painstaking and devoted the labour, the more delicious is the moment when that timid little scurry of water licks away the first few grains. You never see a child cry to see it, do you? When he sees a turret topple, his only regret is that it wasn't higher. By the way, I think I may be able to do rather well by your philatelist. What would you say to Lord Denarius? Or whatever he might choose to call himself? Hmmm?"

I was shocked to silence for a while.

"Surely that is hardly possible?" I was feeling a strong flush of the revulsion that Fanny Buller had commented on. I was also feeling a degree of alarm. I had perhaps not made things perfectly clear with McLaren. Perhaps he had an exaggerated – a hugely exaggerated – idea of the amount of funds available. A barony was a very expensive thing. I could have made a long list of chaps who'd paid a hundred thousand. Prices had fallen very much from the peak, but I had never considered that the scheme I had put to the Bullers would cost Barony money.

It was probably the only time in my life that I came close to saying "steady on, old man."

"I'm amazed that it would be possible, even for you, to arrange that!" I said, "but even if it were, the funds wouldn't go to it."

A slight impatience flickered across his face.

"Never mind the money. It'll be the same as a K."

I was as awed as any child watching the tide eat at the ramparts of his sandcastle. In this case, however, the tide or some other powerful force appeared to be building the sandcastle, which was even more impressive.

"I'm almost alarmed at what we might have set in train here, Alastair. It is becoming a bigger thing than I imagined. Certainly a more conspicuous thing and that's what worries me. Won't people be rather inclined to ask 'who is this chap?' I'm not quite sure that's what we want."

"Certainly they will ask. And we'll tell them that he is the descendant of a second cousin of the Earl of Oswestry whose title was extinguished by attainder at the time of James the Second. His Majesty may be inclined to forgive and forget and restore the family to dignity."

"Is any of this true?"

"Oh, I'm inclined to think something like it is probably true of anybody you stop in the street. If breeding is what you're looking for, the English aristocracy have been pretty spectacular breeders through history. But in this particular case it's demonstrably true. Roughly."

"Really? How did you turn it up?"

"I sent a genealogical person along to Somerset House. Certainly our Mr. Seymour can claim some kind of fairly distant connection with Seymours of rather more glory. But all that is by way of scaffolding. The thing is, you were absolutely right: the King is frightfully keen on philately. I believe that he may think it fitting to elevate the fancy in this way." He raised his glass and smiled. "Let's see if it can be done."

News of Edward's engagement to Marina Tyrrwhitt was given prominence in most newspapers. The couple were photogenic, very rich and clearly in love. The country was in the grip of depression and unemployment; in the further-out parts, some of her citizens were starving; abroad, as we used to call the rest of the world, dictators were strutting and reviewing their arms. The engagement of Edward and Marina, then, was just the sort of story that editors wanted to print and readers wanted to read. For a season the couple were very much in a spotlight. Congratulations came in from all quarters.

Edward put a letter in front of me, having found me at my rooms in Pimlico.

Dear Mr. Buller,
The announcement of your engagement to Miss Tyrwhitt is very pleasing to hear about. Please allow me to join the hundreds who must now be urging their congratulations upon you. All the pictures and stories in the newspapers are, I hope, very gratifying to you, even though you are so much used to being in the public eye. They show that you and your bride-to-be are held in great and widespread affection by the public.

Clearly, you are beginning a new chapter of your life, a chapter that I'm sure will be very happy one. In the new state of affairs, you may no longer wish to continue with your investments in philately. If that is so, I would quite understand, and perhaps it is time to bring our affairs to a conclusion. Let me know when it would be convenient for us to meet. I'm sure we can tie up any outstanding matters in a way that will be perfectly, and finally, satisfactory all round. Awaiting your reply, I am, as ever,

Your humble and obedient servant,

Jeremiah Seymour.

"What's your opinion, Verdon?"

"Until you pick up a snake, Edward, you're inclined to think his skin must be very slimy. You are surprised to find that it is pleasantly smooth but perfectly dry. Mr. Seymour's manner is so pleasantly smooth it is shocking to remember what extraordinarily slimy stuff you are handling. I rather wish he'd cut words out of a newspaper."

"But what does he mean? Does he mean what I take him to mean? Do you suppose?"

"You take him to mean that he's offering to return your correspondence for one last, large consideration?"

"I suppose that's it."

"Well, he may mean it. But he began by suggesting that he'd return these things to your keeping after one first, small consideration. What has he done that should make you believe him now?"

"Nothing. You're right."

He leaned against my mantelpiece and prodded the coals with a poker in moody absorption.

"One can't help thinking there could be an end to it, though. By way of a simple piece of business, I mean. Pay him enough."

"There is no such thing as enough. You're about to be married. You would prefer a clean, blank page. He knows how your thoughts run. His letter suggests that he understands perfectly how you are placed and that he's prepared to accommodate you like a decent chap. Well, of course. Like most blackmailers, Seymour is a decent chap who'll do the decent thing. Is this beginning to sound ridiculous? It should."

"Of course. He'll play me for all it's worth. What do you suggest?"

"I think it's time to try Mr. Seymour's steel."

He looked at me, his elbow on the mantel and his eyes

flickering with reflected firelight and, also, with a certain doubtfulness.

"How?"

"Write to him and tell him that your interest in philately has waned. Tell him . . . tell him that you have learned of certain developments relating to philately – and especially to his position in the trade – and it all leads you to review the importance of the portfolio he holds. Tell him you've found out one or two interesting things about him. It'll rattle him a bit. He'll think it's bluff, probably, but he won't be entirely sure. He won't quite know what to make of it and he certainly won't do anything too precipitate. Now's the time to rattle him a bit, because, oddly enough, he thinks he's in a rather better position now that you're marrying Marina. And, as it happens. he isn't."

"I don't follow."

"That's because you haven't spent the time I have thinking about your affairs, Edward. You're too busy. Look, he thinks he's rather well placed, right now. Before this, he only had one bullet to fire. Now he thinks he has two. If you don't pay up, he can send some incriminating billets doux to Marina. Now, while she might break off the engagement, she won't tell the world. So your career isn't ended and Seymour still has the big bullet and you're properly cowed."

"I can follow his thinking all right, Verdon. And to be honest it seems sound. It's yours I don't follow. You say his position is weaker than he thinks."

"And it is. He has two bullets, but they have to be fired in order. There's no point firing the big one first. That gives us the advantage of knowing exactly what his next move will be if we push him into making it. That is the greatest of all advantages. It is the winning advantage in any game you mention."

"It might be a winning advantage if one had a weapon with which to riposte."

"We will have. For now, it's enough to make him circumspect and keep him a little rattled. If you play chess, and unexpectedly offer a piece for the taking, your man will look about the board a long time, rubbing his nose, before he takes it. He won't fire the bullet that would cause Marina to break the engagement, not until the last possible moment before the wedding. Of course he won't, because what he really wants is the money. Then of course, if he does pull the first trigger, he'll find the shot was a dud. That will give us even more time."

"What do you mean by a dud?"

"I mean it won't work. If he sends her one or all of the letters you ever wrote to Richard, she won't break off the engagement."

"Please, Verdon, don't gamble with things like that. Marina means . . . You know what she means to me."

"I'm not gambling, Edward." I did my best to look feline and composed, "I'm not gambling because I have been very careful to fix the race. From stable lads to Jockey Club as Alastair McLaren would say."

"How have you fixed it?"

"Marina already knows that you were in love with Richard, a long time ago when you were hardly more than boys, and that you wrote some exquisite but embarassing letters."

"She does not."

"She does, Edward, because I told her. I told her before you were engaged. She's a very intelligent woman."

"You bastard."

He turned from the fireside and picked up his hat and coat on the way out. I heard the slam of the front door.

There was no need to explain my actions to Edward. His emotions, with which you cannot argue, would subside, then his brain would take over and he would see the argument for himself. He would be able to reason it out just as I had. Probably, there would be no need for either of us to mention that particular matter again. In the meantime, I wished to hear from McLaren. Our plans were, by their nature, forced to adopt a certain timetable. Honours are published at particular times of the year. Once it was apparent that a bargain could be struck, Buller money would go into a special coffer kept by McLaren's party. Then, Seymour's name would appear on the list that went forward to Number Ten. The list had next to be formally submitted to the King. The King was not expected to find fault with the list. Letters would then be sent to those whom it would now please his Majesty to recognise or elevate. These letters were – are – to their recipients, uniquely thrilling. They inform you that His Majesty is minded to confer upon you such or such an honour. The writer asks you to confirm that you would be minded to accept it . . .

The recipients are not expected to find fault with this letter.

There is only one thing that has ever given me much more than a moment's regret about not being rich. Of course, for the greater part of my life I've been lucky enough to enjoy most of the things that come from being rich. Sometimes I've been hard up, and there has been no one at hand to open a bottle of something good. No matter, I've been content to drink water, treating it with respect and serving it to myself in the best available vessel. Plain water has given me great pleasure. There are all sorts of things money can't buy, and all sorts of things you don't need money for, but neither list includes bespoke shoes. The thing to envy most about the rich is the shoes on their feet. I am told that everybody's feet are of a slightly different size, right from left. If you're rich, so are your shoes.

In a momentary flush of good fortune I had once been to St. James's and had my lasts made. By the time the shoes were made, the tide had turned and I'd been obliged to borrow the money to settle for them. Since then, my lasts had been in store. I am told they are still.

It was a few weeks after my conversation on the terrace with McLaren, as I was walking up St James Street one dusty afternoon, that I saw him coming out of the shoemakers. I thought of my beautiful lasts, cellared somewhere deep within, and felt a pang for them.

McLaren was hurrying but, seeing me, he caught me by the elbow to make me walk a few paces with him.

"Can't do the ermine for your chap. The barony was pushing it a bit, I suppose, and certain chaps looked askance."

"I'm sorry to hear it," I said.

"Would have been a rather good trick if we could have picked it up, but never mind."

"Ahh, but Alastair . . . For you this might be just part of the rubber. For me it was rather an important trick. I'm left with no game to play at all."

"Not at all, old chap," he said, pausing at the kerb and stretching a hand to attract a cab. "Got him a Bart. That'll do, won't it? Rather good, a Bart."

He climbed aboard his taxi and was gone into the traffic of Piccadilly.

I rolled it about in my mind. Sir Jeremiah Seymour (Bart.) It could hardly be improved on. It only remained for this proposal to be put to Seymour himself. "His Majesty commands me to inform you . . ." Once he was engorged with the honey of those words it would be time to draw his sting, and it would hardly be difficult to do. I admit I was looking forward to it, beginning to rehearse the moment, or various versions of the moment, in my mind.

I could not hasten the next step of the operation, but I wanted to see how Seymour's sense of self-importance was coming along. He had, lately, been putting on weight. His jowls were sleek and pink and shiny and his manner was inclining towards a certain pomp. The whole principle of my plan had been that he should start to think himself somebody, and he was responding splendidly.

My feet – the feet that I had been reminded were not quite perfectly shod – were irresistibly drawn to Seymour's shop.

I would like to have told you that Seymour grew much fatter and sleeker as Sir Jeremiah Seymour (Bart.); that he became an international authority in his field and Life President of the International Philatelic Society; that he was invited to sit on Royal Commissions for this and that. No doubt he would never have been quite fully accepted into society, but he would have enjoyed many good dinners. He would, I hope, have been too intelligent to put himself up for clubs at which he would have been blackballed and so would not have been often snubbed. His son, as a man whose father was a baronet, would have been acceptable to the snobs. I would like to have said that Seymour died among his roses in Brockenhurst a few years ago and that his son, an habitué of somewhere called Annabel's, was recently named by an actress as the father of her child in a brief scandale involving minor royalty and a famous and spectacular bankrupt. All of this – or something like it – should have happened. To be honest, I've never been strictly sure what 'gang agley' means. I get the drift, of course, but does it mean that one's plans don't work out at all, or that they might work out in ways one didn't expect?

There were now two assistants at Seymour's and it was a a little time before the proprietor could be fetched to attend to me. When he came into the shop he gave the impression, by the abrupt way he put on his glasses, that it was an annoyance to have been called out. When he recognised me his manner changed in a moment.

"Mr. James, I am delighted that you have called. Would you care to step into my office?"

He installed me in the more comfortable of the chairs and offered me sherry, which I declined with an explanatory glance at his clock.

"May I press you again by saying that I'd like you to drink to my good fortune?"

"Have you done some good business with stamps or are you getting married, Mr. Seymour?"

We laughed a little.

"You might say the former. And the latter may not be altogether out of the question. Please join me. Because, let me be frank, I also wish to ask a favour of you."

I let him fill me a glass.

"I'll have to fill you in on certain things. You know that I write on matters philatelic for a certain newspaper?" He seemed to have forgotten that I had suggested his nom de plume. I nodded and murmured. "Well, I can only put it down to that, really. But some time ago I received a call from an address not so very far from here. One might say THE address not so very far from here." His eyes twinkled with pleasure. His lips glowed moist as he relished his sherry and something more besides. "I was asked to make a certain part of my stock available for the perusal of His Majesty." He looked at me with satisfaction, waiting to see the impress his words would make. I did not disappoint him.

"That is surely very flattering, Mr. Seymour."

"I will admit that I was indeed flattered, Mr. James. I put together the items mentioned and some other things, treated myself to taxicab and went, as and when I'd been told, to the Palace. Do you know . . ." He laughed. It was a boyish, self-deprecating laugh, meant to convey that he had not in any way become vain or lofty, despite the distinction conferred upon him. "When the taxicab drew up at the gates, I really didn't believe the policeman would let me in. My main thought was how I would be able to face paying the driver when he'd brought me home again. But the policeman did let me in. I couldn't resist giving him a little wave. Felt foolish the moment I did it, of course, but the fellow actually gave me a salute. I can't tell you, Mr. James, how grand one can feel being saluted by a policeman. Perhaps you know, of course . . ." He looked at me. I shrugged a sad denial. He carried on. "I was met by a secretary – or possibly he was an equerry, I wouldn't really know – and led what must have been half a mile. I didn't have to carry my wares, you'll be glad to know. A couple of footmen did that. Then the equerry explained to me that what I had brought would be taken to His Majesty, who would give it his attention as soon as he was able. I was to be at hand, in case His Majesty wished to raise a query. And I was just left there. No tea. No sherry. Just left. The fellow said I needn't worry about being kept too long because His Majesty was a stickler about punctuality and that sort of thing and didn't allow people to take up more than their allotted time. So I waited and looked at the furniture and the pictures – all very good, I'm sure, but I'm no expert. After half an hour the chap came back, the footmen fetched my bits of stock and I was ushered back the same half mile or so and out of the door. I had to walk back past the policeman and a lot of guardsmen and look for a cab. Altogether, the strangest afternoon of my life."

"Did His Majesty not buy anything?"

"Oh yes. A list had been made out. I sent everything round the following morning. Got the cheque a week later. I'm rather sorry to say the King does not sign the cheques. He ought to, oughtn't he? Quite a lot of people wouldn't cash them, I daresay. Signed by a fellow called Parker. The thing is that I've been called a few times since then, and the King has favoured me with one or two other little orders by post."

"I'm extremely pleased for you, old chap. Didn't I urge you to get out of that dingy little place in Holloway? Can you imagine you'd have been saluted through the Palace Gates if you hadn't taken my advice?"

"I've always been glad that you urged me as you did, Mr. James. It was exactly what was in my own mind, of course, but a word at the right time is so often the spur to action, don't you find? It was very much the right word at the right time. And I thank you for it."

He raised his glass in my direction. "And now I'd like to ask you for another word or two of advice, if I may?"

"Please do," I said.

"His Majesty has favoured me with his custom. What do you know of the possibility, the likelihood . . . What does one do, I mean, to get the Royal Warrant?"

"Have you asked the King's secretary?"

"Do you know, I haven't dared."

A lion and a unicorn. These were more than enough honour for my purpose. A lion and a unicorn gilded over the shop or in a tracery of gold leaf on the pane of the door. This was the prize. Enough to let Seymour feel it come within his grasp and then to let him see the fabulous beasts pale and recede in his imagination.

I made a call to McLaren.

"How does one apply for the Royal Warrant, Alastair? Assuming you've sold some cabbages to the King?"

"I should think you ask for it. I don't know, I'm not a bloody shopkeeper. Why do you ask?"

"Because he's sold some twopenny blues – and a rather beautiful album and a special sort of magnifying glass and I don't know what else – to the King."

McLaren laughed.

"And the bugger could have been a Bart."

The rest was something of an anticlimax. It turned out, as McLaren had said, that one simply applied for the warrant. One wrote to the Comptroller of The Household, or some such, applying for the warrant to use the Royal Coat of Arms with the words 'by appointment'. There was a short answer, if the King was not disposed in your favour, and a much longer one if he was. It was longer because it laid down exact terms and conditions and caveats concerning the use of the Royal Coat of Arms, all of which you'd expect. In sum all this amounted to the condition that the recipient must in no way besmirch the Royal Arms or bring them or their associations into disrepute. It may be that a word was laid in the ear of the Comptroller of the Household who was probably a member of one of McLaren's many clubs but, whether or no, Seymour had his answer and it was the long one.

To mark his new grandeur he had the whole of his shop front rebuilt. The expense was great but the result was splendid. Above the shop where his name had formerly been painted, it could now be seen in gilded relief. When first done it looked as if the shopfitters had made a mistake. They had failed to get the thing properly in the centre. The space left over, of course, was to receive the Royal Warrant. This was an elaborate piece of construction and painting, as Seymour was sparing no expense, and it all had to be made by craftsman in the City. The splendid crest was still in their workshop when the rest of the shop was finished and the paint drying. So, for a while, the shop front looked a touch asymetrical and awkward.

This was the time that I paid my last visit to J.Seymour (Philatelic) Ltd. I went in the company of a strikingly handsome young lady.

"Miss Tyrwhitt," I said, "May I introduce you to Mr. Seymour. Mr. Seymour, this is Miss Tyrwhitt. Perhaps you know of her."

Seymour's composure wasn't quite up to it. He said nothing, nodded slightly and lost something of his sheen. I suggested that we withdraw into his office. He stood aside and ushered us with a gesture but still without a word. It was clear that simply, physically, he could not speak. Marina sat. Seymour and I remained standing.

"You will be wondering, Mr. Seymour, what you can possibly do for Miss Tyrwhitt."

He made no answer of any kind, so I continued.

"Just as you and I collect stamps, Miss Tyrwhitt collects letters. She would like to collect some letters from you."

Seymour's cheek's had become peculiarly mottled and he was trembling the way one does after a close brush with a nasty accident.

I admit that what happened next owed something to a taste for theatricals that I've never quite been able to outgrow. There weren't so very many workshops that were accustomed to the specialist sort of work, so it had not been hard to find the one doing the job for Seymour. I had taken it on myself to make arrangements for delivery of the work. The thing had been waiting in a van round the corner when I was introducing Marina to Seymour. One of Seymour's assistants tapped on the office door.

"The men have come with the coat of arms, Mr. Seymour. It really does look very grand, sir, I must say."

"Very good. A moment." Seymour had found his voice, but

not the note of pleasure that surely should have been his at this moment.

"Oh, Seymour, old man. Let us go and see your splendid Warrant. It will cheer you up."

We went out into his shop. The craftsmen were showing a little impatience.

"If it's all the same to you, sir, if you can tell us exactly how you want it, we'll get it up there straight away. We've to be back in Holborn by four."

I held up a hand.

"A moment. Mr. Seymour may not be wanting the goods."

"S'all the same to me, sir. We've just got to get on, that's what it is, you see." He looked at a piece of paper in his hand. "S'up to you what you want."

"How true," I said.

"It's all paid for," said the chap in overalls.

I turned to Seymour.

"Not quite, is it Seymour, old chap? It may have to go back yet."

Seymour led me back into his office. With hands that were still trembling he opened his safe. It was a large, capacious safe, adapted for the fireproof storage of documents and, in this case, the more valuable parts of Seymour's stock. From it he took a bundle of letters tied with tape and handed them to me. I restrained him as he was about to close the safe and pulled the door wide. He made no effort to prevent me. He had lost his tautness, somehow, like a balloon that had started to deflate. There were other bundles of letters. I looked from him to them.

"Please," he said.

I was in the happy position of being able to dispel a certain doubt in the minds of several other men, besides Edward Buller. Some of them were known to me, some not. It made no difference. In all cases I arranged for an anonymous return of the letters. I suppose the recipients put it down to a sudden urge of decency on the part of J. Seymour, by appointment . . .

Not so very many years later I stood on the leads of a roof

with Alastair McLaren, not far from Seymour's shop, watching the searchlights sweep a sky made red by fires, and hearing the explosions of bombs. We were both a little drunk and neither of us cared if we were blown to smithereens. We certainly weren't going to go down to shelter or into a tube station. I had offered myself for military service but no one seemed in a hurry to take me up on it. McLaren, as I later found out, had been drafted into counter espionage, but at the time he was claiming that the war had nothing to do with him other than as a spectacle. We didn't even have proper fire-watchers' armbands. From the East came a tremendous explosion of the type we had learned to recognise as a mine. The flash showed us the clouds of Hell in the sky over London.

"Some sandcastle. Some tide." said McLaren.

For a long time we watched and listened without speaking. At last the all clear-siren sounded.

"Look, I'll be in the Café de Paris – if it's still there of course – with Lucy de Windt and Tommy and few people tomorrow night. Why don't you join us? There's something I want to talk to you about. Something has come up that might interest you. By way of work, I mean."

I was late turning up, the following evening, and the Café de Paris wasn't there any more. Alastair wasn't there any more, or Lucy de Windt or Tommy or Al Bowlly, who'd been singing to them. A bomb had fallen through the entire building from top to bottom to burst in the middle of the dance floor. Not far away, half the street where Seymour had his shop was hit. Not Seymour's half. His windows were broken and the horn was blown off his unicorn, that's all.

Hello to Berlin

I have in front of me an item I clipped from a newspaper a few years ago – the date scribbled on the corner is December, 1969. It describes a curious piece of theatre.

'The guard was changed last night at Spandau prison. In the searchlight towers, the watchers of one nation handed over their vigil to the watchers of another with the same grim little formalities that have occurred every month for a quarter of a century. One detail only has changed: there is nobody to watch – except each other. Their boots rang on the cobbles and the sound echoed through a thousand empty cells. Rudolph Hess, one-time deputy of Adolf Hitler, the last and only prisoner of Spandau is sick. They're forwarding his mail to the British Military Hospital. The star of the show – in fact, ladies and gentlemen, the only member of the cast – is indisposed. But the show will carry on without him.'

Beside it, because I keep it in the same manila envelope in my makeshift filing system, is a handwritten copy of a memorandum that I wrote in 1945 on the first night of peace in Europe. It was addressed to the Prime Minister with copies to nobody.

Straight away, let me tell you that I did nothing brave or bold in the war and not too much, I hope, that was bloody. My circle of friends, on the other hand, was quite bowed down under the weight of medals and bars. It was lucky for me that modesty and self-deprecation were the fashion among heroes, because that was all I was entitled to wear. Now that such a lot of time has passed, and so many heroes are laid to rest, I'll make a small boast. My little corner of the war was the one part of the field where we – I mean we British – outplayed the opposition from start to finish. There was some reason for thinking, in my little department, that we'd done rather a good job, but on VE night I went to bed early and alone.

I did not get a night's sleep. There was unfinished business on my mind and, anyway, the noise of a party – somebody rolling out the barrel – made it hard to sleep. At three o'clock, I got up, made a mug of tea with rum in it, and settled down to write my memorandum.

To: Prime Minister.
From: Capt. V.James.

However eager the Russians are to have the Prisoner known as Rudolph Hess stand trial with the other German leaders, it would be better to deal with him in some other way. Our line of argument might well be that he effectively ceased to be a member of the German government when he flew to this country in 1941. At that time his country was not at war with the Soviet Union. Treaty relations existed between the two nations. There can, then, be no case for submitting the prisoner known as Hess to the interests of Soviet Justice, or to any judicial process in which the Soviet Union may play a part.

Should the Soviets insist, despite this embarassment, then a valid plea may be entered that the prisoner is unfit to stand trial. His mental state has deteriorated during his time in captivity. He has bouts of depressive illness attended by episodes of amnesia and confusion. Dr. Delaney is sure that these are genuinely pathological and my own observations lead me to agree. The prisoner's symptoms may have been made worse by the efforts of mind required by the training and educational aspects of his treatment while in our custody. If a clinical term must be coined for his condition, we may call it Uhlsdorf's Amnesia. A plea of unfitness along these lines should be prepared in terms that the court may accept. The prisoner may thus be dealt with more conveniently without embarassing the Soviets."

I scribbled in the margin afterwards, in pencil: "Patients suffering from Uhlsdorf's Amnesia are inclined to think they are someone else, and blot out certain contradictory parts of their own memories."

When the time came, a submission setting forth the plea that I suggested was prepared and advanced on behalf of the prisoner at the Nuremberg court on the thirtieth of November, 1945. I could not have foreseen that the prisoner would then dismiss his counsel and beg leave to address the court in his own behalf. He admitted that he had certain small mental difficulties, but claimed that his previous assertions of amnesia had been lies and that he was, in fact, perfectly fit to stand trial alongside the chiefs of the Nazis still living.

I had better fill you in. In nineteen forty, Alastair McLaren had said something vague about finding war work for me to do. He'd suggested meeting at the Café de Paris after which we were to go on somewhere. I was held up in Pimlico, though I was trying very hard to get away, because I really did want to meet Alastair. The idea of dancing and listening to Al Bowlly was appealing, too. In an uncertain world it is important to take some trouble over pleasure.

Before I could get there, Alastair and Al Bowlly and many more had gone on somewhere else for the last time and the Café de Paris had gone with them. During the days and nights that followed I drank a lot. I wanted to be angry and I tried to weep. The fact that I was simply not in the fight did not help. Nobody wanted my services. I had put my name forward in various quarters where people I thought of as friends were in a position to pull strings. I still had no job. It was not easy to come to terms with the idea that I might, after all, be quite useless. I had that feeling very strongly as I walked into St. George's for the memorial service that we held for Alastair and Henry Wendell and the others who'd been killed that night. I felt so useless, in fact, that I stayed in my pew as the church emptied afterwards, so that I could wait for everybody else to go. I didn't want to hear the questions, "what are you up to?" or "who are you with?"

So I stayed in my pew under the pretence of lingering prayer, listening to the murmur of greetings and conversation outside the church. When I could hear only the traffic in Hanover Square, I got up to leave. I found that I was still not quite alone in the church. One other straggler remained. I passed him on the way out but he caught up with me just outside the door.

"You're James, aren't you? My name's Ross."

We shook hands. I had the impression of having seen him before and said so, apologising for my forgetfulness.

"Friend of Alastair's. Colleague in a way. Are you doing anything for lunch?"

As it happened I was engaged for lunch.

"Can you telephone and put the thing off?"

I looked at him with some surprise. When a stranger suggests with quite that confidence that you break an engagement, he's either a lunatic or he has something serious to say. Ross didn't seem to be a lunatic.

"Can I take a short cut?" I asked him.

"To where?" he asked, slightly surprised.

"To the point in the conversation where you may be about to suggest there is something I might be able to do for you."

"How do you know I'm going to suggest that?"

"You waited for me. Either that, or it just so happens that you and I are coincidentally matched for piety. Doubtful, though, as piety wasn't what kept me in the church. Next, you are a colleague of Alastair's, and you are proposing to have lunch with me. Alastair said he might have something for me. Something to do."

"At this rate we can probably skip lunch. You've been looking for a job. I might be able to find you something. What do you suppose your answer would be by the time we'd had lunch and I'd told you as much as I was going to tell you?"

"I have a feeling that wouldn't be very much anyway."

"As it happens, no, it wouldn't be."

"Doesn't make much difference. The answer would be yes. I want a job to do."

"There could be an outside chance. We'll have lunch another time." He put a calling card in my hand. "Come and see me, ten o'clock tomorrow."

He turned and strode off across the Square, holding his hat against a little flurry of wind.

At ten o'clock the following morning I walked the short distance from my rooms to Vincent Square and rang the bell at the address on Ross's card. Not being sure that the bell was really working, I also thumped with the tarnished brass knocker. The house seemed to be a private dwelling with nothing to distinguish it from the rest of the terrace. White shutters were drawn across inside the windows on the ground floor and the glass was taped against blast. There was a basement with a railed area in which someone had dumped a tangle of barbed wire. The door was opened by a woman in a tweed suit. She had glasses and nicotine stained fingers and didn't pause to listen as I introduced myself.

"Up the stairs to the room straight ahead of you."

There was no name on the door and it was not a very cheerful room. It was waiting to become somebody's office. There was a brown desk with a linoleum top standing not quite in the middle of the floor. A chair to match it for utilitarian ugliness was lying on top of it. A green filing cabinet stood obscuring part of the window. A telephone sat on the floor at the end of a skein of black cable. The walls were covered in a dispiriting greenish wallpaper, extremely grubby around the light switch. There were no pictures or decorative touches of any sort.

I waited for ten minutes or so but nobody came. I went back out onto the staircase and listened. A certain amount of muttering came from behind the next door along the landing, but I could make nothing of it because a typewriter was chattering away on the floor below. I went back down the staircase and opened the first door I came to and found the tweed-suited woman typing in maestoso style at a black machine not much smaller than a grand piano. She had a cigarette pushed to one corner of her mouth, with her face screwed up to keep the smoke out of her eye. She showed no interest in my arrival.

"I believe Mr. Ross is expecting me," I said.

"Colonel Ross," she said and kept on typing.

"I wonder where I might find him?"

"Up the stairs to the room straight ahead of you."

"You are quite sure of that? There is nobody there at the moment."

"No," she said, "that's because you're down here."

I went back to the room on the first landing. There was still no sign of Ross. The chair still lay on the desk.

I took it down and moved the desk to a more convenient position where it enjoyed what light came through the heavily taped window. The filing cabinet was more awkward to move and had to be waddled on alternate corners to a better resting place. Out on the landing I had noticed a coat and hat stand. It looked more purposeful when I had put it in the corner by the door. Once I had hung my hat and coat on it and hooked my umbrella on the thing, it lent a pleasant air of occupation to the room. I wiped the dust from the seat of the chair and sat at the desk. The drawers were all empty, but for one, which contained several sheets of ruled paper and an incomplete maintenance manual for a motorcycle of some kind. The ruled paper I squared up and put on a corner of the desk. The motorcycle manual I passed up as the first offering to the waste paper bin. If the telephone had only been connected to an exchange, I'd have been ready to set myself up in any business that took my fancy.

The woman in the tweed suit, still wreathed in smoke, had reached a very animated passage of typing when I opened her door again.

"Why does the telephone not work in that room?"

She stopped typing and took the cigarette out of her mouth, which allowed her face much needed relief from contortion.

"They're supposed to have done the telephones last week. You can't say when they'll come. They say there's a war on."

"See if you can't chivvy them up. And if there's any gas . . ." I glanced at the far corner of the room where a kettle stood on a gas ring, next to a tea pot, "I should be extremely glad of a cup of tea."

I looked at my watch, which, by reflex, made her look at her own, confirming that it was time for a cup of tea. "If you could send one up. No sugar. Milk if there's any. You seem to have rather a lot of chairs."

A row of bentwood chairs scraped the walls on two sides of her office.

"We need them," she said. "From time to time."

"Then call on me if you should run out," I said, lifting the least rickety looking chair and taking it with me.

I now had an office, a desk, a hatstand, two chairs, a wastepaper bin and the prospect of a telephone line. By retrieving the too hastily discarded manual from the litter bin, I was equipped to offer advice on certain aspects of motorcycle maintenance. It was beginning to look as if I might, at last, be able to make a contribution to the war effort. I knew from many conversations I'd had that London was then stuffed with people in very similar offices making just about the same contribution. The difference was that they had more paperwork to show for it.

The woman in the tweed suit brought me a cup of tea accompanied by two biscuits in the saucer.

"Colonel Ross telephoned. His apologies, but he's tied up. He'll try to see you this afternoon, if you can wait."

"If there's still a war on this afternoon, I'll wait."

"About the tea. We have a little fund. To buy the sugar and biscuits and so on. Everybody puts in sixpence a week."

I gave her sixpence. The tea was disgusting but I drank it on principle. Once you're in the tea fund, you're part of the establishment. At lunchtime I walked up to the Army and Navy stores and bought a calendar, an inkwell and a blotter. In a bric-a-brac shop near the station I found several pictures. One was a portrait of Admiral Beatty in a quite respectable frame. Another was a stirring depiction of the battle cruiser Lion steaming full ahead at Jutland that must have come from the same house clearance. There was also a large watercolour of Tintern Abbey. One of the odd advantages of the blitz was that it was easy to bargain down a price with a man who couldn't entirely dismiss the idea that his stock might be blown to oblivion in the night. I got the lot very cheaply, together with a few nails and some wire to hang them.

H.M.S. *Lion* I put up behind my desk, the Admiral on the wall opposite. I used my shoe for a hammer. Tintern Abbey took a little thinking about. I tried several places and eventually settled for the piece of wall that first met your eye on entering. It wasn't the best light for the picture but the effect was the most congenial and welcoming. When I'd finished, I thought of McLaren's beautiful Tabriz rug and wished I could throw down one to match it. I couldn't, of course. Some of us have to settle for linoleum.

I was writing a letter when Ross came in. Naturally, he came in without knocking but in an instant he stopped.

"Sorry old man," he said and immediately left, closing the door behind him even before I looked up. I heard his footsteps out on the landing; heard the door to the next office open and a brief exchange of voices.

His footsteps returned and passed down the stairs. The sound of typing was arrested for a few moments and then Ross's footsteps came back up the stairs. The door was opened and it stayed open. Ross stared at me.

"Whose is this bloody office?"

"This morning it didn't seem to be anybody's. This afternoon it seems to be mine. Do come in."

"Yours, is it? And what do you do in it?"

"I'm waiting for somebody to tell me. Just like half the chaps in London from what I can make out."

Ross sat on the bentwood chair, threw his feet up on the desk and carried on staring at me while he took a cigarette case from his pocket.

"Smoke?"

I declined.

"Do you mind?" There was a certain sarcasm in his tone.

"Not at all," I said. "Use the bin for an ashtray. They don't seem to have supplied me with one yet."

He lit his cigarette and drew on it a few times.

"There's someone coming to see me in a little while. Someone who doesn't know me. So for this afternoon's exercise, as you've occupied my office, you might as well carry on being me. You're Ross."

"What's he coming to see you about? See me about, that is?"

"Find out. And don't make assumptions. You speak German, I gather?"

"I read it better than I speak it, I'm afraid."

"Been to Germany much?"

"Not much, no."

"Why the German, then?"

"Because there is really no such thing as exact translation. I was reading philosophy at the University and rather a lot of it was turned out by Germans. So I learned German."

"You read Greek as well, then, do you?

"I don't suppose that will be very useful in the present emergency, will it?"

"I don't know what will come in useful, but don't mention philosophy too often. The War Office doesn't have much time for that sort of thing. They might decide you're an intellectual."

"I'm hardly that. Anyway, I ride and shoot and so forth so my disguise is pretty well complete."

I heard the light patter of a woman's footsteps outside. Then came a tap on the door and I realised what Ross had meant when he advised me against making assumptions. She was striking enough to look at, not at all fragile, well shaped and with an expression that either challenged or invited you to look twice. Without needing to look twice you were aware of the sensual mouth and the abundance of brown hair that framed her face. She wore her clothes with the air of a woman who expected her clothes to be noticed. I remember only that she wore a suit with a slim skirt and that her hat was made of velvet.

I introduced myself as Ross and introduced Ross, with an air of intentional reticence, as "a colleague".

"You haven't met, I assume," I said looking from one to the other. They both shook their heads.

"This is Miss . . . forgive me . . ." I turned to her.

"Fanshawe. With an E. Diana Fanshawe." They shook hands and then she sat on the bentwood chair proffered by Ross and waited. Ross wandered to the window.

"Well, Miss Fanshawe. What is it that you think you might be able to do for us?"

She rearranged her legs and adjusted the hem of her skirt by a millimetre or two, then turned on me a softening look from her brown eyes.

"I thought I was here for you to tell me."

I was aware of Ross resting indolently against the window-sill and reaching for his cigarette case. I couldn't see whether he was smiling or not.

"Then . . . tell me something about yourself."

She crossed her hands on her lap, leaned back a little and looked up as if wondering where to begin.

"Don't start too far back. What have you been doing lately?"

"Lately I've been in a long run at The Prince Frederick."

"Of course," I said. And of course, I should have known. She was an actress. I could not, though, remember having seen her, or recall what had been playing at the Prince Frederick.

"You had rather good notices in that, didn't you?"

"The play had good notices. I took over from Hermione Street quite well into the run. I imagine you really know all this. The man who told me to come here certainly did, so why shouldn't you?"

"Don't put too much faith in . . . liaison, Miss Fanshawe. We can make no assumptions at all, just at the moment."

"To be quite honest, when your man spoke to me I wasn't sure whether I was being arrested or recruited."

I took a leap, not entirely in the dark. Ross had been scheduled to see me in the morning and Miss Fanshawe in the afternoon. The interviews might not have been entirely unconnected. Ross knew, probably, rather a lot about me, but he'd only brought one thing to the surface.

"Do you speak German, Miss Fanshawe?"

"I hope it's not an offence."

"Not at all. How do you come to speak German?"

"I had a German governess."

"And you have spent time in Germany?"

"Am I being investigated?"

"Of course. Everybody in the country who had a German nanny or a governess is being brought in and interrogated."

"It must help to pass the time."

"You spent time in Germany?"

"You must know all this, I spent holidays in Germany as a child. I have Hessian relations. A Hessian is a kind of German, I cannot deny it."

"Miss Fanshawe, I'm not suggesting that it is improper to have German relations. Or even to speak German. I'm in rather the same boat, but in my case it's worse. I have German friends. Relations, after all, you can't choose. To have friends is much more suspect."

"Then why are you talking to me at all? It's such a rigmarole."

It seemed a good time to invent a reason.

"Miss Fanshawe, you will be aware that very few English people speak German, or indeed, any foreign language."

"I am certainly aware of that. It seems to be considered rather un-English."

"You probably know that in Holland, for instance, practically everyone speaks German or French and quite commonly both as well as Dutch."

"I believe so."

"Holland is, at the moment occupied. But any conversation between Germans is likely to be perfectly understood by any Dutch man or woman who might happen to overhear it. Imagine for a moment that a German invasion were to succeed or partly succeed here. Things would be rather different, wouldn't they?"

She raised her eyebrow to mark that she was following me perfectly.

"Exactly. The Germans could walk about chattering their darkest secrets pretty well with impunity. They could hold strategic planning meetings in the bandstand in Hyde Park. Compared to the Dutch – or even the French – any potential British resistance is off to a poor start. Now do you see why this department ..." I waved my hand deprecatingly about the room I had furnished, "why this department wants to contact intelligent and, erm, reliable men and woman who understand German?"

"Yes. Yes, I do." She leaned forward to my desk. She was following my thoughts quickly, almost more quickly than I could invent them.

"Your talents and training as an actress might be as useful as your command of German. Simultaneously useful, if you can imagine that?"

"I can."

Ross straightened himself from the window sill, walked to the door, where I could see him but Miss Fanshawe could not, and shook his head. He made a gesture with his hand that clearly meant I was to bring the interview to an immediate close.

"Then for the moment, Miss Fanshawe, may I say that it has been delightful to meet you and very encouraging to speak to you. This department will be in touch. Thank you for coming."

Behind her, Ross opened the door and smiled.

She turned in the doorway, very much as an actress would turn, making an exit.

"It has been very interesting, gentlemen. I'm only disappointed to think that you won't be getting in touch with me again, after all."

"Will we not?"

"No. Because when the swines do try to invade us we shall kick them where it hurts. They'll never walk into London the way they walked into Paris. Still . . . it seems you know where to find me, if and when you want me. Good day."

Ross closed the door behind her.

"Where did all that guff come from?"

"I made it all up as I went along. Still, it was rather a good guess about the German, don't you think?"

"Yes it was."

Ever since I had begun the interview with Miss Fanshawe, Ross had been toying with an unlit cigarette. He now lit it and wreathed himself in smoke and his own thoughts for a while.

"Why don't we have some tea?" I suggested. "I've put sixpence in the fund, after all."

Ross looked at me, not very amused.

"I'm not sure what I should make of you, James. You've usurped my office and, either by a fluke or some kind of unhealthy divination, you seem to have absorbed my thinking processes."

"I just thought you'd be ready for a cup of tea."

"All that stuff about the British resistance was on the nail. What you said to Miss Fanshawe was a pretty good summary of why both of you are in my address book."

"Do I win a goldfish or a coconut?"

"I'm not sure what you win. Probably a bullet in the back of the neck. If the Germans do invade we need to have a body of credible collaborators that British intelligence can run. I imagine that Miss Fanshawe might get onto . . . erm . . . intimate terms with a top Hun. And you seem to be able to worm your way in anywhere. Starting with my office. Sixpence in the tea fund, eh?"

"Look here, Ross: if you like, I'll explain why I made free with your office."

"You needn't bother. I may be in military intelligence but I'm not stupid. You were brassed off waiting, and it was a way of saying you were tired of it and that you really did want a job."

"Thank you for understanding. The pictures cost me five bob. You can have them if I get a job."

"You can keep them yourself. You can keep the office, too, though I should think you'll have to share it before very long. You've got a job. Get the tea up and we'll talk."

An inclination to asthma had, so far, led the armed forces to turn me down as unfit for service. Now it was necessary for me to be subject to military discipline. Within a week I had the King's commission despite my unreliable respiration. For administrative convenience, I was put on the same list as chaplains, and therefore immediately enjoyed the rank of Captain. The only advantage this rank afforded me was that in the case of any serious lapse on my part, I would have the privilege of being shot by my employers rather than hanged.

Having war work to do was, for the first few days, very like not having war work to do. I went to my office in Vincent Square every morning and before long had given the nicotine-stained Mrs. Ambrose another sixpence so that I should have tea to drink. I got onto nodding and greeting terms with the two men who worked in the office next door without knowing what they did there. Ross brought papers and assessments – that is, guesses about the enemy's plans to invade – that I was to read and digest. I was in the dark about what to do with the information once I had digested it.

"Look James," said Ross one afternoon, "your job is either top priority or it doesn't matter a toss. Get your imagination working on ways in which British resistance might be sustained, co-ordinated and directed in the case of enemy occupation. There is, at present, nothing under this heading on the War Office shelves. Our friend McLaren believed that your mind was fashioned on somewhat oblique lines. What I know of you inclines me to agree. The point being, if meeting the Germans head on doesn't work we may need to resist them more obliquely. Carte blanche, dear boy. Let us know your thoughts. Nobody else has any."

While Fighter Command was fighting them in the air, and Winston was telling us that we would fight them on the beaches and the landing grounds, I was imagining how we might, if it came to it, fight them in the cellars and the sewers and by stealth. It did not take long for this job to seize my imagination and I worked on it night and day. In a very short time I had written thousands of words for a fairly small readership. I defined what I hoped were good general principles and then outlined proposals for the command and control of an organisation that had no command and control centres, many of whose forces would be without military training or understanding. For this part, if no other, Captain James was better qualified than most. I'll admit to being pleased with the general introduction, which I wrote last of all. It was a short but closely reasoned chapter that I entitled 'The Objects of Resistance.' I began by addressing a fundamental question and my first paragraph was headed, 'Why Resist?' I am told that Mr. Churchill tore the pages out and threw them away. "It is a question we need not answer," he said, "because no Englishman will ask it."

All the same, I'll admit to being so pleased with my efforts that I was almost disappointed to see the threat of invasion recede. This didn't put me entirely out of work: the job was simply turned inside out. I was told to imagine that I had been given exactly the same job by the Abwehr, and to think how German resistance might be organised in the event of an Allied invasion. In nineteen forty one this possibility was so remote that my work could not really have been called urgent. I began to pester Ross for work from a slightly more active file.

"The trouble is finding a niche for you, old chum. You have no military expertise, so you're not going to be much use assessing intelligence coming in – or, more especially round here, going out."

"I thought the idea was just to stop intelligence going out, not assess it as it went."

He lit another of his cigarettes and I pushed him the ashtray I'd had bought especially to cope with his visits to my office.

"Of course that's what the brass wants to do. Stop anything getting out. But there is another way of looking at it. Imagine for a moment that we have scooped up an entire network of German spies. Then imagine that we are smart enough not to shoot them. Then imagine that they are smart enough to be turned into agents working for us. What have we got?"

"Assuming the Abwehr hasn't rumbled what's going on then you've got a pretty good way of wrong-footing the German High Command, haven't you?"

"Exactly. You can use this network to feed the enemy misleading information."

"For so long, anyway," I said, "until they realise that it's duff gen."

"You have touched the thing with a needle, old chum. If all you feed them is duff gen, they'll rumble it pretty damn quick. It follows that you have to feed them a carefully balanced diet. It means you have to let them have some of the real stuff."

I sat back to think about this. It was a slightly alarming reversal of the ordinary assumptions.

"So, if you had scooped up a whole network of German spies, you're saying you'd want to give them real, valuable military information to pass on to the Abwehr?"

"Yes."

"Information about our operational dispositions?"

"Yes."

"Information, say, that might help the Luftwaffe select its targets? I assume that's what spies are supposed to do. How about that?"

He looked at me very steadily.

"Yes."

"My God."

"You've hit a very good point with Luftwaffe targets. It is possible that we could, by selective dissemination of intelligence, lead the Luftwaffe to attack a particular target, one particular town, one city, rather than another. Yes."

I think I may have whistled at the implications.

"It might be phoney information, but they would be real bombs," I said. Not that he needed me to say it.

"We would be sacrificing pawns. Sometimes more than pawns. But if it protected some more valuable piece on the board . . ."

I stayed silent for a while. So did Ross. He simply smoked and looked at me.

"Do I assume that we have scooped such a network of German spies?" I asked him.

"Funnily enough. Not everybody is quite certain about this, but I am. I know in my bones that we've got them all. We are at the moment running all or just about all the German spies in England."

"Why do you think that?"

"They had a few chaps in place before the war and we rumbled them. They weren't really very good, but we turned them. One of their chaps has been transmitting quite cheerfully from a fairly comfortable cell in Wandsworth Prison for over a year. The point at first was to know what sort of information the Abwehr was asking for. Tells you a lot about what they're planning."

"I see that. How is it we seem always to have been taken by surprise, then?"

"Don't be sarcastic, old chum. Not all of us were. And since then, there's been more of an inclination to believe what some of us say. The point is, the Germans suddenly decided they needed a lot of information very quickly before they invaded, so they threw in a lot of agents in a hurry. They all had beautiful papers which they used with the greatest confidence because they'd been forged according to details sent back by their chaps in situ. They just didn't know that the particular situ was Wandsworth Prison. The beautiful papers made them very easy to bag. They weren't very well trained, they thought their job would be over in a few weeks anyway, and they weren't hard to turn when they'd been picked up. One or two were genuinely dedicated, very tough chaps. They had to be executed, in accordance with the Articles of War. Which, I suppose, only served to make the Abwehr believe that everything was running pretty well as per normal in the spying business. And, by the way, I'm not very sure I should be telling you any of this."

"I'm still wondering why you are."

"Because what we have in our hands is an instrument for deceiving the enemy. In the end, when we get a chance to kick back at the bastards, good deception could be crucial to the success or failure of a big attack. As long as we can keep the instrument in tune until then, of course. Now it's up to other people to sort out what kind of real gen to give them. I want you to put your mind to ways, means and ends of deceiving the enemy. Let's start to work on a few essays in deception, so that when we have to do it on the night, we won't be doing anything we haven't rehearsed. Am I making sense?"

"Perfectly."

"Then let me have your ideas. Not on paper. You remember the day you moved yourself into this office?"

"Yes."

"I think that's when you got this job. All you did was to arrange the furniture and put up a picture. But when I walked in through that door, I walked straight back out again saying, 'sorry'. Obviously I'd made a mistake. It wasn't my office. I was absolutely deceived. In the same circumstances, I think anybody would have been. But all that happened was that some cheap furniture had been arranged to accord with one set of expectations rather than another. Think the same way and call it strategic deception."

I was in the deception business. I didn't realise at first that I had joined an elite unit. As I began to meet the rest of the department, I was rather flattered. I worked with men who marshalled and deployed entirely imaginary forces, sometimes whole notional armies – there were several of these in the end – and they were among the most able and intelligent officers I met in the course of the war.

I reported to the Twenty Committee. The Twenty Committee was subordinate to the W Board. The W Board was account-able to nobody but itself, not even the Joint Services Intelligence Committee. Disinformation is too delicate for discussion. Few regular officers knew of our existence, but among those few we were deeply distrusted. It was as well that not many people knew about the Twenty Committee and how it came to be called that. The Roman numeral for twenty, you will remember, is a double cross.

Sometimes the notional units and forces that we put into the field were pure phantoms of the cipher world of intelligence. Their existence could be inferred from rumour; given foggy substance by decode and interpretation; proved by intercepted radio transmission. They were creatures of the ether. Sometimes the business was much more like putting on a pantomime or amateur theatricals. Sometimes it was all of these things to-gether. I spent a night in the spring of nineteen forty two sitting up with an amiable German spy in Wormwood Scrubs. At the proper time I listened to him relaying a fragment of information he'd picked up by diligent eavesdropping of careless talk. There was a moment when he had difficulty reading my handwriting and needed a little prompting before picking up the staccato theme again on the morse key. The following day, a reconnaissance Messerschmitt appeared over certain acres of Sussex. We know that the Messerschmitt pilot found a concentration of armoured vehicles. As he knew where to look, the attempts at camouflage were easily penetrated. Clearly, there was a field of tanks and other motorised units crudely disguised as small farm buildings, perhaps pigstys, and agricul-tural machinery. In the same cell in Wandsworth, two nights later, I was playing chess with my friend the German spy. I was going to beat him, but he was putting up a more astute defence than I was used to seeing from him. We had to put the game aside unfinished when the time came for him to tune in to the Abwehr for instructions. He was to pay particular attention to gaining information and, especially, possible embarkation in-structions of the armoured unit mustered in Sussex. What unit was this? Under what command? Details of armour type? Were the vehicles fitted with desert filters? I'm sure he managed to send back snatches of useful stuff. On the ground in Sussex, a collection of small farm sheds was demolished and farm vehicles were sent back to their proper business the following night. A bonfire was made of an amount of timber and painted calico. A tank flimsily disguised as a corn thresher is hard to distinguish from a corn thresher flimsily disguised as a tank. It depends which you're expecting to see.

In my working hours I was a backstage worker in a rather peculiar theatre of war. In between times I was becoming familiar with the backstage world of Shaftesbury Avenue.

I had been put in a position that made it easy to get in touch with Diana Fanshawe again. If I asked her to lunch – which I did – it was a certainty that she would not turn me down. It helped that she was under the impression that it was her duty to accept. She believed that she knew why I was asking her to lunch and she believed that I was called Ross, so there was a certain amount of unstitching to do. It wouldn't have been necessary, had I not found that I was thinking of her a good deal.

Dear Miss Fanshawe,
You were kind enough to call in at Vincent Square and talk to me about a long term theatrical project. It's beginning to look as if the show may not be going ahead but, all the same, I wonder if we might meet to discuss other possibilities. May I suggest lunch any day you like next week?
Yours,
James Ross.

Dear Mr. Ross,
I should be delighted. Will I be? Say where.
Yours,
Diana Fanshawe

Dear Miss Fanshawe,
I hope you will be. You deserve to be. The Maison Blanche?

It was still possible to dine out well in London. As the war
went on and rationing became more stringent, the menu became
shorter. The first time I went with Diana to the Maison
Blanche, they were still able to offer something passably like the
pre-war à la carte. By the war's end we would simply sit down
and eat whatever they could put in front of us. The other
hospitable pleasures remained, heightened by shortage and un-
certainty: the sparkle of white linen, the uncorking of good
wine, the easy formality of good waiters with familiar faces, the
breeze of cheerful conversation around you, the sound of your
own voice saying unfamiliar, banal and foolish things. Falling in
love.

I began, as I had to, with the confession.

"There is something I must get out of the way. My name
isn't Ross. That was a quite meaningless deception, not aimed
at you."

She did not seem in the least put out.

"What is your name?"

"James. That's the second bit. The first bit is Verdon. It's a
slightly back to front sort of name. Use any bit of it you like."

"I think I prefer Ross. Ross was a Colonel. Are you?"

"I'm only a Captain, I'm afraid. Not a very convincing one, I
know, but I am."

"Captain James, then."

"Please don't call me that. I am a Captain, but I don't even
know how to salute. It's just so they can court martial me if
they feel the need."

"I can't call you Mr. James. It makes me sound like the
housekeeper. Verdon will have to do."

"Thank you."

"I should tell you that my name isn't really Diana Fanshawe."

"Is that a stage name?"

"I'd stick to it if I never worked again. It's a great improvement."

"On?"

"Dorothea Tremlett."

"Diana suits you better. I'm not sure about Fanshawe."

"Call me Diana, then."

"She was the patron Goddess of slaves. Did you know?"

"I thought she was simply the huntress."

"Oh, she was certainly that. There was a special cult of her worship at Aricia, with a temple deep in the forest and a high priest who got the job by slaying his predecessor. He kept it for as long as he was strong enough to avoid going the same way."

Her eyes lit with delighted laughter.

"I didn't know that. It sounds like an excellent arrangement. One would never have a doddery high priest."

"I suppose that was the idea."

"If one were a big enough star, the casting of leading men could be arranged on similar lines."

"Who would I have to kill at the moment?"

"Do you have ambitions to go on the stage?"

"Of course."

"At the moment you wouldn't have to kill anybody. I'm not in a show."

"No leading man at all?"

"None."

"A high priest anywhere?"

"No. One or two altar boys who turn up occasionally, I think that's all."

"Diana, I can't quite believe that. London is full of handsome and heroic young men who believe they may be dead tomorrow. They'd fall in love with a town hall clock if it struck at the right moment. You are not a town hall clock. You're extremely beautiful and you're marvellous company. They must be clambering over each other."

She put her hand over the top of her wine, the way someone

might who was declining the offer of more. She was silent for a while.

"Yes. A lot of them will be dead tomorrow. Some of them already are."

"It was rather a crass thing for me to say. I'm sorry."

She shook her head abruptly and stared at her glass for a while. Her features displayed no emotion. She had the composure you might see in a carving from Egypt and the light that shone from the white table linen, sculpting her face, only heightened the impression. I felt stupid. It's not how you want to feel when you have fallen in love.

Let me tell you about Dieter Maria Uhlsdorf, the dyestuff salesman. In nineteen forty he was working in a prison bakery in the North of England and had become quite an accomplished baker of bread. Dieter Maria's job had been to sell German dye to the English cloth industry and his English was excellent. He had been taken off the street in Leeds and interned in 1939. MI5 was slow to be convinced that Dieter Maria was innocuous and he had been interviewed intensively. In the end, it was clear that if he was a spy, he was nothing more than a low level intelligence gatherer, like any other businessman. He was punctilious and obliging, and an unshakeable admirer of Adolf Hitler. His faith in the inevitable triumph of the Third Reich ran to complacency. It made him laugh to reassure his jailers that he would put in a good word for them after the British surrender. It made him laugh, but he was not joking. Apart from that, he had not much to say that was amusing or interesting. The most interesting thing about Dieter Maria was that he looked exactly like Rudolph Hess.

There was no remark on the file to comment on this resemblance, but then it was not the sort of thing to interest an MI5 officer, whose job was to counter the enemy's efforts at spying. As long as a man was of no further use to the enemy, he was of no further interest to MI5. If he was to be of any use, he became our pigeon. In my job of trying to anticipate how a possible German resistance might operate I had set aside time for conversations – not more than that – with a cross section of internees and POW's. I thought it would be of use to gauge what you might call the spirit of the citizen in the Third Reich.

Perhaps I'm not very good at this sort of thing, but I spent a week travelling round the country not learning very much that was useful. There were some very dull conversations, one or two quite lively ones, but very few informative ones. I spent an interesting hour with a Jewish professor of philosophy whose internment on the grounds of his German citizenship was an embarassment that I'm glad he did not ask me to explain. The trip was keeping me away from London and away from Diana, and I almost cancelled the last day of it in favour of taking a convenient train back. I would have done, but for sharing a ministry car with a Group Captain who turned out to be a friend of Edward Buller's.

"Don't bother with the train, old chap. A very dodgy means of transport these days. Get yourself out to Wissington tomorrow ack emma. I'm flying back to Northolt. We'll keep you a seat."

Getting myself out to Wissington the following morning turned out not to be easy or cheap. The Group Captain and several other officers had already left, having set off earlier than intended to keep ahead of weather. He had left no message concerning any late arrivals. Getting back into Leeds from Wissington meant hanging around for transport. It also meant missing the best train and eventually wasting a day and a night making a journey that the Group Captain had made in not much more than an hour. On the other hand, I was stuck for a while in Leeds, with time to do my duty, and so I met Dieter Maria Uhlsdorf.

There was a photograph on his file, of course, but as with all such photographs, the subject didn't look like anybody at all and certainly not himself. In the flesh the resemblance to Hess was instantly striking. After some pleasantries and inquiries as to his comfort, I commented on the resemblance.

"It has often been mentioned. We are exactly the same height also."

"Really."

"To the millimetre." He said this with a grin of pride. "Der Stellvertreter perhaps weighs a few kilos more than I. But I have been mistaken for him in Germany. It is very convenient if you want a good table."

"You impersonated the Stellvertreter?" I laughed and widened my eyes. He laughed and shook his hands denmurringly.

"Oh. Nothing of that kind. But I have found, you know, if I was going into a bar, some ordinary place, they would say to me 'You look just like Hess!' But . . . if I was going into some better kind of place, some place you would call very snob here, expensive, you understand, then the people would not be so sure that I was not really Hess. They would not dig me in the ribs, ja?" He was clearly pleased with his mastery of English idiom, because he leaned forward, patted my knee and repeated himself, laughing. "They would not dare to dig me in the ribs. Just in case. The pity was, I could not so often afford these places."

How often does it turn out like this? Quite by chance you meet a word, a man, an idea for the first time. The next day, in another place, going about other business, the same word or man or idea jostles you again, from another angle entirely. I got back to London and went straight to my club to bathe and eat. Diana had left a message with a telephone number. A male voice that made me think of polished amber answered my call. When its owner went to find Diana I was left listening to a distant chatter of other mellifluous voices. Music was playing.

"It's a wonderful party," said Diana. "Hop in a taxi."

"It sounds like a very theatrical party. I hear evidence of tremendous elocution around you."

"Come. You'll like them. They're great fun."

I went of course, but I went with misgivings. I was tired and felt dull. Diana's theatrical friends were, I could hear, lively and sparkling. I should cut a rather poor figure and not be very entertaining when what I wanted to do was monopolise Diana's attention. But I was in love. I went.

The first few minutes after I arrived at the party didn't do much to put me at my ease. Diana was nowhere in sight and while there were many familiar faces, they belonged to people I didn't know. Meeting people whose appearance is famous – whose appearance may be the basis of their claim to fame – is something I still find a little embarassing. The camera may not steal the soul, but it makes an odd bargain with believability. The first time I met Olivier, it was very much like being introduced to someone claiming to be Hector or Agamemnon. When he, in turn, introduced me to Vivien Leigh, he might as well have said, "Do you know Helen? Helen's over here from Troy."

I learned to enjoy the company of Diana's friends, but I wasn't enjoying it that night. I was out of it and what I overheard offered no way in. The anecdotes that made other people hoot meant nothing to me. The nicknames brought nobody to mind. I heard whole sentences – speeches – that were obviously English but might as well have been beautifully articulated Latvian for all they conveyed to me. Before long, their laughter was nothing but braying, and their obviously beautiful faces were just as obviously hideous. Somebody had been kind enough to give me a drink, a curious mixture with bourbon in it, and then had been heartless enough to find me uninteresting and move away.

A middle aged woman in a Chanel dress passed me on her way into the room. Her face was entirely unknown to me, a circumstance that was, on this occasion, almost an invitation to converse.

"I wonder if you've seen Diana Fanshawe anywhere?"

"She's in one of the bedrooms with Dorian Lisle."

I must have looked dismayed.

"They're getting ready."

"Getting ready for what?"

"To perform. Go up."

She was hailed from another quarter. Her face was transformed into a rapture of recognition in which, suddenly, there was something familiar after all, and she was gone across the room.

I went the other way, through the hall and up the stairs. On the first floor I could hear Diana's voice.

A bedroom door stood a few inches ajar and I tapped on it. I heard Diana laugh.

"Is that five minutes? We're almost there . . ."

I was reluctant to walk into a bedroom uninvited. On the other hand, I was not inclined to stand outside a bedroom door calling her name or announcing my own.

"Are you dressed?" was what I settled for and it felt foolish.

In a moment the door was opened by a stranger, but the stranger laughed, put her arms around my neck and kissed my cheek.

"You came, I was afraid you wouldn't. You sounded so tired, poor lamb."

She was a stranger, of course, only for a moment. But it was a long moment. The woman who answered the door to me was Eva von Braun. She took my hand and drew me into the room. A man was sitting before the mirrors of a dressing table pencilling his eyebrows.

"Have you met Dorian Lisle?"

The man at the mirror turned. Everything about him was familiar. The dark hair parted on the right and falling diagonally down his brow, the absurd square of moustache. The small clenched mouth relaxed into a warm smile, however, and he stretched out his hand.

"You must be Verdon," said Adolf Hitler, "Diana talks of absolutely nobody else these days."

I sat on the bed with my peculiar drink watching the actors add final touches to their own and each other's make-up.

"Now they've closed the West End theatres again, we have to keep ourselves amused, you see," said Lisle, trimming gauze from the moustache.

Diana laughed.

"As long as we keep other people amused, darling, we shall be serving in our way!" She turned to me.

"Dorian has been told that he's a key actor and they don't want him in the forces. It's his duty to keep up morale."

"I was deferred – we all were – until the end of the run. When the theatres went dark again, thought I was off to the Navy. Not likely! They won't have me at any price."

"I'm sure it's a disappointment to you."

He turned on his stool. Adolf Hitler addressed me in the voice of an English actor of the classical sort. His way of speaking was a kind of vocal topiary.

"As a matter of fact it is, old chum. Few things would please me better than the chance of being a hero. Or do you think I'm funking it?"

"I'm sorry if I've given you that impression. I didn't mean to."

"Look, old man. Heaps of people have volunteered very cheerily, and they've never in their lives done anything or known anything that's made them sick with fear. They don't know how they're going to be when that moment comes. Well I do know, because I've been sick with fear plenty of times. I mean sick. I mean vomiting sick. I mean standing in the wings smelling my own bile. On a first night in the West End, one does, you know. But one goes on. You don't really think there's an actor in town who couldn't manage the swagger to the recruiting office and a bit of flourish with his signature?"

"I have given you the wrong impression Mr. Lisle, for which I apologise. Again."

Dorian Lisle laughed uproariously then, and slapped my thigh. "Oh, your face!" he said. "Your face!"

The two of them were laughing and I began to see the joke.

"Oh Verdon," said Diana, "Dorian may be the most shocking coward in history, but he's not quite that pompous!"

They both roared with laughter again. Dorian Lisle put away sticks of make-up in an Upmann's cigar box and turned to me again.

"I'm sorry, old man. I embarassed you but one can't resist it. What do you think of Adolf?"

He struck an expression, quite suddenly, that was wholly Adolf Hitler and rose to his feet. His eyes burned, shooting their gleam towards some distant horizon. His lower lip worked with nervous energy, like a man mentally rehearsing the first words of a speech to thousands. With his hands crossed flat in front of his fly buttons, he took a half step forward and then raised his right hand, not in the full ceremonial version of the salute, but in the comfortable lower case version that Hitler often used by way of return. The hairs stood on my neck. I wondered what the effect would have been on Dieter Maria.

The little sketch with which they entertained us was hilarious but its success will not survive description after half a century. They entered as the newly wedded lovers from The Merchant of Venice, gazing into each others eyes "in such a night as this . . ." No, it is best not brought back. It was perfect at the time. Now it could mean hardly anything. Much of it, anyway, was an extemporised dialogue with wits in the audience and impossible to recall. It was, at all events, hilarious and brought them tremendous applause. I was learning that next to being applauded the thing that actors like best is the opportunity to display how generously and beautifully they, too, can applaud. Afterwards, Diana rearranged her hair and make-up to look like Diana again, but Dorian Lisle stayed at the party as Adolf to the end. He removed the moustache finally because it interfered with the pleasure of drinking.

I walked with Diana back to her flat as there were no taxis to be had.

"Your Eva von Braun is a great triumph, you know. You should tour it."

"Oh we are going to. Didn't you know?"

"I don't quite follow."

"There's a rule now. For actors like Dorian. Their call-up is deferred but they are all going to do things for ENSA. It's Entertainments National Service. Going about with little fit-up companies to cheer up the troops."

"I think I've heard of the idea."

"Well Dorian's worked up a little revue. Noel Coward has written something for him, too. He says he'll take it round the sort of places where you just can't, with the best will in the world, put on a serious play. Dorian would put on a play in a telephone box, so he must be thinking of some God forsaken places indeed." She looked at me sidelong. "Bullety sorts of places, too, you know, if it comes to that."

"Diana, I'm sure your Thespian friends are quite as brave as anybody else. I honestly have the greatest admiration for people who'll stand up and entertain us and make us laugh when the bombs are falling. My friend Bowlly died doing it, when he could easily have said, "Right oh. Off to the shelter." Or even, off to America. I thought he was immensely brave and what he was doing was important. Now will you let me off?"

"You're sweet, Verdon. But then, you're an actor, too, aren't you?"

"Am I?"

"You played Colonel Ross to perfection."

We talked of other things and arrived, too soon, at the steps to her apartment.

"Am I going to kiss you goodnight?"

"I hope so," she said, "but not here. I don't sleep on the step."

Waking up for the first time with someone you love is like waking up in a new life. If this observation is trite, I don't apologise. I remember looking at her hair on the pillow and watching the pulse beat in her startlingly naked neck, just beneath the translucent Meissen of her ear. I saw her shoulder turn in her drowsiness and the down on her cheek catch gold from the sunlight and gild her alabaster skin. I remember seeing all this even though I also remember that the blackout curtains were closely drawn and the room was entirely dark. Love, I suppose, is light.

The bombing raids were still frequent in London. We had not become inured to them because you never do, but we had become too accustomed to random destruction; to the arbitrary disappearance of the place we happened to be going to, or past or through. Picking your way to work past and sometimes over rubble still hot from the flames, was now too customary to seem defiant and heroic, as it had at first. It was just an ordinary irritation.

Walking to Vincent Square from the tube the morning after I had taken Diana home, and feeling as buoyant and delighted with the world as I was, it seemed especially unimportant to be walking past rubble that yesterday had been something I knew. I passed a cluster of shop girls standing on the pavement opposite the shop where they no longer worked, as it wasn't there any more. A hundred yards away, the street was blocked by barriers that meant an unexploded bomb and added the length of another two streets to my walk. The shop girls were waiting, I suppose, for someone to tell them what they should do. While they waited, their heads were together and they talked in excited, hissing sentences. They were talking about a girl who'd managed to get herself pregnant. The extraordinary had become ordinary; the ordinary was as interesting and exciting as ever.

In Ross's office, I tried to put together the bits and pieces and make an idea out of them.

"Up in Yorkshire I talked to an internee. He makes no bones about his sympathy with the Nazis, thinks they'll beat us in short order. Seems to think the only reason we haven't shot him in the neck and tossed him in a pit is because we know that, if we do, we'll be for the high jump when the Swastika goes up the flagpole. The really interesting thing about him is he looks exactly like Rudolph Hess. By a sort of coincidence I went to a party with Diana Fanshawe last night . . ."

"You went to a party with Diana Fanshawe, did you?"

"As it happens – don't look like that, Ross . . ."

"Have you been abusing your position, James?"

"I took her address and telephone number from government records, yes."

"Well done. Carry on . . ."

"Diana and a friend, an actor fellow called Dorian Lisle, of whom you probably know, performed a satirical entertainment in which he played Hitler and she played Eva von Braun. They really were very funny. More to the point, they were absolutely convincing. They were playing for laughs, of course, but some of the best laughs came when this chap Lisle played Adolf dead straight. The laughter was of a different kind, if you know what I mean. The way you'd laugh if someone were decapitated in front of you and you were hoping it was a trick and not the real thing. Quite eerie."

"It sounds wonderful. I'm glad you get to such frightfully good parties. Quite envy you, but why do I need to know this?"

"Well, in between meeting the Hess fellow and being entertained by Adolf and Eva, I was stuck in Leeds with time to kill waiting for a train. So I went to one of those little cinemas where they show nothing but newsreels and cartoons. Sat through Movietone a couple of times. I started thinking. The Germans are really much better at propaganda than we are. They've devoted themselves to the subject. We censor the press and the newsreels, we spoonfeed them stuff, yes, but we don't fashion them into instruments of policy with the same ruthless science that Goebbels brings to bear."

"Ruthless science isn't our long suit, laddie, no."

"Goebbels has been using the newsreels for years. He controls them absolutely and the evidence is that he's done it with great success. The Germans love them, because the newsreels, probably more than anything else, told them that Germany was great again. The newsreels brought them the Führer's message and the Führer's soul. Certainly the Führer's image and the Führer's triumphs."

"Don't waste any more time telling me how important the Hun thinks newsreels are. Get on."

"After this I'm more or less busking, so bear with me. As I see it, the ordinary German citizen has been taught to place great faith in the newsreels. If the instrument is so powerful in

Goebbels' hands it follows that the same instrument, in the hands of Goebbels' enemy, could be equally powerful."

"I'm starting to get interested."

"It would be a once and once only deception, probably, but if you could adulterate or corrupt the medium in some way, you might have a profound effect on public morale. Choosing your moment carefully, it could be a great advantage."

"Adulterate or corrupt. Tell me how . . ."

"I imagine the distribution of films around the cinemas is managed in much the same way in Germany as it is here. In each city or region there's a place where the reels are exchanged for passing round the circuit each week. Goebbels' central unit, or somebody, sends out so many copies, on such and such a day, to each of these exchanges. Imagine that a certain shipment is substituted, at the exchange or some other place down the line, for alternative newsreels . . ."

". . . Adulterated or corrupted newsreels. Yes. But you haven't quite told me what that might mean."

"I'm not entirely sure. There are a number of possibilities. These alternative newsreels must seem to be genuine, but imagine − just say what if − in the middle of one of Herr Hitler's tremendous harangues things went deliriously agley."

"Agley?"

"Like the best laid plans of mice and men . . ."

"In English we say awry."

"What if the headline story were, I don't know . . . Hitler makes momentous speech to the Deutsche Volk. Martial musik. On comes Hitler, Eva von Braun by his side, holding his hand perhaps. Hess is there, just a little behind him, looking glum. Imagine Hitler making the same sort of speech that our own dear late King Edward made on the radio not so long ago. 'The game's up. I'm chucking it. Make your own arrangments. Thank you for your support. I'm going off now with the woman I love.' Something like that."

Ross looked at me. His expression was impossible to read. He toyed with his cigarette case, tossing it and catching it.

"Look Ross, I'm not a scriptwriter but just go down to Bourne End and throw a brick. It'll hit one and bounce off another. They could come up with dozens of possibilities. It would depend on the effect you wanted to produce. If Hess suddenly started to talk like Donald Duck, I think it would go down well in the middle of one of Goebbels Glory-of-the-Reich specials, don't you think? On the other hand I think we could be more subtle than that."

"I get the drift. Doctored newsreels. Effect on civilian morale."

"They could be used to stimulate uprising. If it were to be done in Holland or France, timed right, it might be the starting pistol for civilian uprising and sabotage in the prelude to invasion. In the case of the Germans it might be just a matter of lowering morale. Then, it might just help to shake some of them out of their infatuation with the snake charmer. Call it the Fat Dutchman effect."

"Enlighten me."

"Göring once said 'If a single English bomber ever gets through to Berlin, you can call me a Fat Dutchman.' I gather that our little air raid on Berlin didn't add up to much in terms of damage done, but there are Germans who now call Göring the Fat Dutchman. I think that means it was worth the effort."

Ross went through the ritual of lighting a cigarette that always accompanied his process of reflection. When he was suitably wreathed in smoke and had shaken his match vigorously and ground it into the ashtray, he looked at me again.

"You think it would be possible to substitute – what – hundreds of cans of film?"

"There is already a mechanism for shifting thousands of cans of film around. I should think it's a job done by fairly low grade labour without any very elaborate security."

"I daresay you're right."

"It's exactly the sort of operation that resistance units are capable of tackling. Much easier than sabotaging trains, or blowing up bridges. It's the sort of thing that could be done by what you might call the man-in-the-street resistance worker. At the crudest it's going to mean waylaying the deliveries, but it would surely be better if our friends were to get jobs in the business. Ideally we need some sympathetic entrepreneurs to go into the film distribution business. I'm sure it can be done."

"I'm going to put this up, old lad. I think it's barmy but that may be a recommendation. Give me a memo. Try to get some idea what it'll cost. Try to make it sound unbarmy and cheap. You never know."

I was in films. Operation Dutchman was warmly approved in the highest circles and given the highest stamp of secrecy. My first act as producer was to have Dieter Maria moved from Yorkshire to a different place of internment. Wormwood Scrubs was more convenient for the studios at Ealing. I still wasn't sure whether Dieter Maria was to be a star or just a very convincing extra, but a man who looked just like Hess and spoke in the Munich dialect hardly needed to audition. My second act as producer was to bring both Diana and Dorian Lisle into my office and bind them formally with an oath under the Official Secrets Act. Diana swore the oath as if checking off a laundry list. Lisle, who was delighted by the thing, conferred upon it an unearthly solemnity. The thing was done in my linoleum-floored office, but Lisle achieved a sonority that made it seem as if he were swearing vows in a cathedral. My third act, under the powers granted to me, was to forbid Dorian to perform his Hitler impersonation at any time or place other than those authorised by me. This caused him a momentary dismay that was dispelled by Diana.

"You realise Dorian, darling, that you've just become a secret weapon."

The idea appealed to him very much.

I wanted Anthony Asquith to direct the filming, but Anthony was already working at full stretch on other kinds of filming for the war effort. Over a drink at Edward Buller's he recommended Percival Atwater and nobody could have been better for the job. Percival, it seemed, had studied every frame of Leni

Riefenstahl's Nazi propaganda films. If anything, I thought him a little too much of an admirer.

"Remember, Atwater old chum, we want to make a newsreel, not Triumph of The Will."

"Don't worry about that. All the German newsreel men are trying to remake Triumph of the Will, anyway."

Atwater was a practical man and didn't confine himself to what you might call the dramatic and aesthetic problems. He had entered into the whole spirit of deception.

"When these things arrive in the projectionist's hands, they've got to arrive in the usual kind of film can."

I must have looked dim.

"Film comes in light alloy cans. They are reinforced by having a pattern stamped into the metal. A projectionist would immediately recognise an unusual kind of can. And the leader would have to be exactly the same kind that he's used to. That's the section of film spliced onto the head of the print for lacing up through the machine, with marks for focussing and synchronising sound and so on. No importance in itself, but a different kind of leader would just make him start noticing things. Really you want the projectionist to grab the can, lace up the film, hit the button and go back to feeling up his girl or whatever the bastards normally do. Because mostly, I swear to you, they hardly notice what they're screening. You don't want them to notice, of course, so all those little details must be as normal as possible."

"Then we need to get hold of some German film cans and so on."

"And the labels and the paperwork and everything. All of that's important. You do all that sort of stuff and leave the film to me."

It was not difficult to get hold of a current German newsreel in a standard issue can. They were screened as a matter of course in neutral Switzerland and Spain. We made British Movietone News available, too, but we didn't get as many takers in those particular countries. The can the film goes out in is a detail that the film producer normally doesn't have to worry about. I was discovering that he already has enough to occupy him. Film-making involves many forms of activity and each of them, however trivial, has a name and is the unencroachable province of a specialist. However simple the duties of the specialist he must have at least one assistant whose function is not always apparent to the outsider. If the film industry set out to play a mouth organ, there would be somebody different to blow down each hole and they'd all have assistants. It would take a week to get through Three Blind Mice, and you wouldn't recognise the tune until a month later when their efforts had been edited together. After a while you begin, dimly, to see why some of this is necessary. At one frustrating moment I exclaimed about it all to Atwater.

"Oh, filming the evacuation of Dunkirk would be easy," he said. "You just have to be there with a camera. Faking the evacuation of Dunkirk so as to film it is another thing entirely and vastly more complicated than embarking an army. And then the light wouldn't be right. And when it was, half the boats would turn up and go away again before the soldiery ever arrived and you'd have to do the whole thing again ten times. But just think how many people it took to arrange the original cock-up. The film industry, cock-up for cock-up, is really much more efficient. You just deliver my Hess for the first day of shooting."

We'd decided our first essay would be to prove the concept. Dieter Maria could hardly be asked to learn lines and act for the camera. He might not be willing and anyway, he was a dye salesman, not an actor.

"Don't give him any idea what we want him to do. Just send him along, but dress him in a party uniform like Hess's. That's all."

A dressing room was made secure with bars on the windows. A spy hole was provided in the panel of the door. I thought all this was going a bit far but the Home Office, in the person of a pertinacious little whey-faced Scottish person, insisted on the precautions. Dieter Maria was brought to Ealing studios in the company of two prison officers. As they had no idea why he was being taken from his cell, they were not communicative and Dieter Maria interpreted their silence in the most ominous way. When he was told to strip, and his clothes were taken away, he became nervous and agitated. I had wanted to explain at least something of our intentions to Dieter Maria, though it would have been difficult to judge quite what and how much to tell him. Atwater, though, was quite sure of what he wanted.

"Don't tell him a thing. If that makes him agitated and uncertain – and I'm sure it will – then that's all to the good. I want him keyed up."

We left Dieter Maria in a state of doubt for an hour or so. This was not an intentional cruelty. It's just the way things happen when you're trying to make even the simplest piece of film. Other problems press themselves on your attention; nothing is ready when you need it to be ready; nothing works the first time you try it, not even an electric light. When they brought him the uniform that Berman's Theatrical Outfitter's had supplied, Dieter Maria began to sweat even though he was wearing only his drawers, vest and socks. He refused to put it on and demanded to see the Red Cross. He got me.

The room stank. The vest clung to his belly, damp with fear.

"What's the trouble, old chap?"

"They are wanting me to wear this uniform. Why?"

"Do you not wish to wear it? It's a National Socialist Party uniform. Rather a good one."

"I want my own clothes."

"Your clothes have been taken away, I'm afraid."

"Why?"

"They are very fine clothes made in Germany. We need them to give to our spies."

"You will have a spy in Germany walking in my clothes?"

"I suppose that's the idea. Not my department."

"Give me ordinary prison clothes, then."

"I thought you were an admirer of the Party?"

"I know why you want to put me in these clothes. You will throw me to a mob."

"That is not the sort of thing we do."

"You are going to shoot me."

"Only in a manner of speaking."

His eyes widened and his lips went visibly dry.

"What are you going to do?"

"We are going to take some pictures of you. That is all. Please put on the clothes."

He wrapped his arms around his ribs and rocked slowly back and forth against the wall with his head dipped to his chest. There was no looking into his eyes. They were pools of shadow under the bony ridge of his forehead and the thick brows.

He made no response at all when I leaned to touch his arm. When I spoke to him in German, he looked up so sharply that his head struck the wall behind him, though he seemed not to notice it. It was the first time I had used German to him.

"Please believe me, Dieter Maria, we do not intend you any harm. You are an internee. You are protected by international law. I am asking you to co-operate. Unfortunately, the Military Intelligence people are not entirely happy about you. They are inclined to believe that you were spying for the Reich. They do not believe that you should be treated as an internee, but as a suspected spy. Do you understand?"

His eyes glowed very white at the bottom of their dark pits. He understood.

"If you will co operate with me, you remain the responsibility of my department, which is propaganda. Which would you rather be? An actor, or a spy?" I had used a word I had not meant to. Actor. Still, it was the other word that absorbed his attention. Spy.

"It is up to you. I will leave you for a few minutes to decide."

When I came back to the dressing room and looked through the Judas hole, Dieter Maria was adjusting his tie. I watched for a little while as he stood taking in his own reflection. The sight absorbed him. An actor would have turned his head this way and that, catching his profile, working an expression. Dieter Maria stared dead straight at himself. His only movement was to stand suddenly straighter and taller to meet his own still gaze. I was looking at Hitler's deputy. So was Dieter Maria. Atwater wanted him to be on edge, so I omitted the courteous tap on the door and walked in impatiently, as if things were going wrong in some way. I gave him hardly a glance before holding the door wide.

"Good," I said. "Follow me."

The moment of grand confidence he'd enjoyed looking in the mirror was gone. I hurried him down the corridors faster than there was any need for and took a roundabout route to the studio. When we finally passed through the double doors of the sound proof entrance Dieter Maria was sweating again.

In the middle of the soundstage was a rostrum, perhaps thirty feet long, swagged with German flags on either side of an enormous central swastika. Above the rostrum was a long speaker's dais, covered in scarlet cloth and bearing the outspread wings of the Nazi eagle in black and gold. Behind it and on either side, everything else was black. Tall flats that might have been scenery were covered with a dull black cloth. The scene was lit only by a bald working light, as comfortless as the light of a prison cell or, perhaps, some even more unpleasant corner of a prison. From somewhere distant in the gloom came Atwater's voice.

"Can you ask your chappie to sit at the dais, please? There's a chair for him."

Leading Dieter Maria onto the soundstage and up behind the dais was like leading a baffled child. I almost took him by the hand. There was one chair behind the dais, not in the centre but a little way to the right. I tried to draw it back to usher Dieter Maria into it, but found that it was fixed rigidly to the floor.

"Just sit him down would you and tell him to wait. Oh and tell him not to get up and walk around. Just wait there till we're ready."

"He understands English, Atwater. I don't need to tell him."

I smiled at Dieter Maria. He tried to smile back. It was just a little clench of his jaw that pressed his prominent top teeth into his bottom lip. He wiped his dense eyebrows with a thumb and then jerked upright as a powerful light came on, dazzling both of us. I patted him on the shoulder with a smile and left him.

I joined Atwater in the preview theatre to watch our first rushes. I was beginning to pick up this sort of jargon. It meant we were going to watch the first prints of unedited film straight from the camera in a room like a very select cinema.

"This may not be riveting stuff, but I'm rather pleased with it. I've just chopped some promising bits together that I wanted Tim to see. Sorry. Captain James, Tim Standish. Vice versa."

Tim leaned across from a seat in the row in front of me and shook my hand. He had thick glasses and smelled of whiskey and cigarettes. Dandruff crowded the slope of his shoulders.

"Tim's the writer."

"Excellent," I said, but perhaps I betrayed something that suggested I didn't immediately have faith.

"Tim has written some wonderfully funny stuff."

"Has he? I haven't seen it yet."

"For the cinema. Films. He hasn't written anything for us yet. What he's going to write depends on what we're about to see."

He pushed a switch on the desk in front of him and murmured an instruction. The lights dimmed in our little cinema and images began to dance on the screen.

In a few moments, the image was of a long dais, swathed in Nazi flags. Seated behind it in what seemed a vast black space was Rudolph Hess. He looked sweaty and nervous. From time to time he looked up against the light with his eyes screwed up until they were just slits in the deep sockets. Sometimes he thought he heard noises and peered out into the gloom at the side of the dais. Once or twice he looked behind him. Gradually, it was clear, he got used to the idea that nothing much was

about to happen and that he had been forgotten about for a
while. He yawned twice and managed to suppress another.
Atwater tapped Standish on the shoulder and they nodded at
each other, without taking their eyes from the screen. Dieter
Maria's hands began to drum a little tattoo. Briefly he began to
pick at something caught in his molars. Then he recollected
that he was sitting under a bright light and was probably
observed. There was an abrupt slash in the film where Atwater
had cut out a lot of time, and then Hess began to pick at
whatever was stuck in his molar again. Boredom had clearly
made him indifferent to observation. Whatever was stuck in his
teeth was not easy to deal with. Suddenly, he gave up picking at
his teeth and it was clear that things other than particles in his
teeth were beginning to irritate him. He looked about, glower-
ing, and sat sharply back in his chair, folding his arms abruptly
across his chest. In the gloom of the preview theatre, Atwater
leaned forward to Standish, who cranked his head back and
they muttered to each other, pointing at the screen from time to
time. Standish scribbled notes continually.

On the screen, Dieter Maria – whom I now could only think
of as Deputy Fuhrer Hess – leaned abruptly forward over the
dais and shouted.

"What is going on here? What is going on? I wish to
co operate. I will co operate! But you should tell me what is
going on."

"Wonderful, wish he'd said it in German, mind." said Standish.

"He does in a minute," said Atwater. "It gets better."

More time had been slashed out of the film. Now the
Deputy Fuhrer hunched forward over the dais, clubbing the
flat surface softly with his fists. Then, in German, he pleaded out
into the world he could not see outside the bright light.

"Please. I just wish to be told what is going on. Why am I
here?" He waited for an answer but no answer came. He called
out again, louder and with hysteria beginning to show. "Why
am I here? Tell me what is going on!"

Standish clapped his hands in pleasure and turned quickly to Atwater, who sat back, nodding and smiling.

"Here it comes."

Dieter Maria stood up suddenly, shouting in German. "This is intolerable! I will not sit here! This light is killing me!"

Atwater's voice amplified very loud was heard on the film.

"Sit down or you will be shot immediately!"

You could see exactly where the voice had come from by the way Dieter Maria's head shot round, his eyes wide and white. He shrivelled back into his chair and stayed still and silent.

"He sits like that for twenty minutes. Doesn't move a muscle. A wonderful piece of film in its way but I can't think who'd want to watch it."

Atwater leaned forward to the button on his desk again. The lights came up and the screen was blank again.

"It's terrific," said Standish. "And the turn, when you tell him he'll be shot, that's spot on. They'll be eyeball to eyeball."

"I had the speaker absolutely on the line, but just to make sure we put a little light on it that we could flash up. Bang. Looked straight at it."

"Well it's a piece of cake, old chum. Your Hess fellow is terrific though, isn't he? Absolutely, Hess to the life. Let's go and do some creative drinking."

Standish was already grabbing his coat and heading for the door. Atwater was getting ready to follow him.

"A moment if you will, gentlemen."

Standish paused with the door held half open. He continued to stand with it held open, like a man in a hurry who might just give me half a moment of his time.

I waited until he reluctantly gave up his grip on the door and allowed it to close. The door made a little automatic sigh. Standish may have done the same.

"Gentlemen. Explain to me."

"Oh right. I can shoot another film with the actors but without your Hess. Except that the actors will be working as if he's there and doing some of the things we've just watched.

Because the camera's fixed rigidly in the same position, I can combine the two into a little drama."

Standish pushed open the door again.

"Tell you in the pub."

"Mr. Standish, will you come here a moment."

With a great display of weariness, Standish left the door and came a few paces back into the theatre.

"This is not something we will discuss in a pub . . ."

"Oh, for God's sake, don't take me so bloody literally, all I meant . . ."

"It's not important what you meant, Mr. Standish. Just understand what I mean. I mean that if you talk, you will be dealt with. You will not be at liberty to talk thereafter."

Standish got the idea and showed it by a weary shrug and a nod of his head. I began to realise why people in the sort of job I was doing tend to become megalomaniacs or thugs. It creeps up on you.

We had a final cut of our motion picture in less than a month and screened it for the W Board. The critical reception was unanimously favourable. As to whether the thing might be in any way useful, opinion was divided. The print was sent down to Dytchley Park, one of the Prime Minister's safe rural retreats, for a private viewing. I was flattered by his request. Then, of course Rudolph Hess knocked the bottom out of the whole idea by misappropriating a Messerschmitt, flying to Scotland and attempting to call on the Duke of Hamilton by parachute. Hess's behaviour was a surprise to everyone and to me a peculiarly irritating surprise. It led to an even greater surprise. I was called to Dytchley Park.

"Captain James. Sit down. If you care to help yourself to brandy please do. I can't be quite so liberal with the cigars, I'm afraid. They are hard to get and they are something of an essential prop. National morale will sink if I am seen to go without one for too long." I helped myself to brandy, though I knew it was stretching Winston's politeness, but the old man seemed to be in an hospitable and relaxed mood.

"I say that to you, James, because you obviously understand the significance of props and greasepaint. I have been impressed by your essay in motion pictures."

"I think I'll count that as a good review, sir. Thank you. Even if it's so much wasted effort by now."

"Deception, deception, deception, James." He communed with his cigar for a while and during his silence I couldn't think of anything to say.

"Deception," he said again, rising from his desk and then crossing the room to gaze out of the window. "The worst of war isn't that good men have to kill. It is that they have to lie and deceive, and these are much harder habits to break. All the same, we must be the better killers and the better liars. Everything I hear about you tells me that you are one of the best and most accomplished liars we've got."

"That is a rare compliment, sir."

"It is, James, because there's a lot of runners in the stakes. And, frankly, I'm at the head of them. You remember my saying, once upon a time, that we would fight them on the beaches and the landing grounds, on the hills and so on . . ? That was a lie. We should hardly have been able to fight them at all. Once the Panzers were ashore, we simply had no weapons that would have stopped them."

"But we would have fought them, all the same, Sir. No lie there."

He turned towards me and smiled. It was a short-lived rueful sort of smile that ended in a shrug.

"We didn't have the weapons to stop them. Not on the ground. But we had some rather good lies. And, if I may say so, some rather good liars. There's a kind of liar better even than you or me, James. Put your lie in the mouth of a fool who believes it, and you've got the best liar of all."

When Winston summoned me to Dytchley Park I don't think it was especially in his mind to treat me to the discourse that followed. He was faced with a question I knew nothing of, and with making a decision whose consequences affected me only slightly, so why did he tell me so much? I can't say. Perhaps it was a necessary part of thinking out the problem.

"Hitler has a fool in the person of Rudolph Hess. He has flown here with a lie in which he believes: peace between Britain and Germany. We need not be detained by close scrutiny of the seven points of his proposal. They amount to a lunacy. It comes to this: we shall surrender, not shamefully, but with the honours of war; our people shall be spared further horrors; we shall then live in peace and contentment as allies of the Reich. Where the French have Pétain, a former Field Marshal and national hero at their head, we shall have the Duke of Windsor, a leader of fashion and our former – now to be future – King. The war-monger Churchill will be sent packing."

I laughed.

"Is the Duke of Windsor aware of the part he is to play?"

Winston did not laugh at all.

"Yes. Very well aware. He has been our fool. The fool through whose mouth this powerful lie has been . . . noised abroad."

He looked at me with the gaze that everybody close to Winston knew and nobody who was not close ever saw. It was not the gaze of the favourite uncle, or the teddy bear or the bulldog. In 1688, his ancestor led the coup that threw a King of England off his throne. The fact came to mind as he gazed at me.

"The Duke of Windsor has engaged in conversations culminating in this proposal."

"Discussions with the Germans? Direct discussions?"

He nodded. It was not easy to take in, but not impossible to believe. After his abdication, the Duke had visited Germany. He had met Hitler and Goebbels and been made welcome. He had enjoyed his welcome and paid compliments to his hosts. All that, though, was before the outbreak of war and, until very late in the day, Hitler had not been short of admirers in England. One might mention that the Bank of England had arranged loans for Germany after Hitler had come to power. Naturally, one does not mention it often. I mentioned it then, together with similar circumstances concerning other people in England who then – as now – drew a veil over company they had enjoyed or opinions they had held before the war. I thought the same veil might be large enough to screen the Duke.

"And, of course, he has a quite natural sympathy for things German, in normal times. His mother is German, after all. He has grown up speaking German as easily as English."

Winston cut me off . . .

"That will certainly have been a help to him in these conversations." The rebuke was in the tone. he gestured towards me with the cigar. "Which took place after the fall of France."

"That does come rather nearer to fraternising with the enemy."

Winston made a sweep with his hand that may have been intended to dismiss my remark or disperse a cloud of smoke. The one mattered as much as the other.

"The Duke made his way, at that time, into Spain and then to Portugal. Countries where these contacts are by no means impossible to arrange."

I began to understand.

"With perhaps one exception, sir, the Duke is the most conspicuously recognisable Englishman alive and not without some importance. It would be fair to assume constant vigilance on the part of our security services."

Winston nodded, but it was as if his mind were really on something else. I believe he was making up his mind how much of the story it was useful to tell me. I carried on with my own thought.

"I assume, then, that he was – how can I put it? – allowed the freedom to embark on these negotiations."

"We made use of his inclinations. We fostered his illusions. We sponsored his . . . I'll use your word . . . negotiations. We judged that it was in our interests for Hitler to believe that the English had no appetite for continuing a war against Germany and to let him conclude that an advantageous peace with

England was in prospect. Windsor, it seems, really does believe these things, so we allowed the idea to ferment in his mind and in German minds together. We may have added more than a little yeast." He laid down his cigar. "We gave large scope to this delusive nonsense before we appointed him to his present duties in the, erm . . ." he groped in the air with his cigar, in an expressive pretence of forgetfulness. ". . . Bahamas. He sits impatiently, awaiting his country's call. You will understand why this deception was in our interests, hmm? Hitler's great aim is the destruction of Russia. He may call it a war against Bolshevism, but it wouldn't matter who or what ruled in Russia, this would be his purpose as it was the Kaiser's: a matter of necessity and, as Hitler sees it, destiny. But he knows that fighting on two fronts is folly."

"He's seen at first hand what that did for the Kaiser, of course. Or, put another way, for the Duke of Windsor's Uncle Willi."

He nodded at me

"But Hitler has done better than Uncle Willi. He has taken the Kaiser's plan – the Schlieffen plan – to second base: France is out of the game. If we would just lie down, he could start to travel East."

"And the Duke has played his part in letting him believe that we would do just that."

"Exactly. Herr Hitler has been making his preparations to travel East for three years. He has a timetable. He must commit his troops very soon. If he delays so much as a month after the snows melt, he runs the risk that his campaign will run into the Russian winter – a subject on which, you will remember, Napoleon has marked all our cards. If he delays another year, the Russians will have increased formidably in strength. The longer he goes on believing in this chimaera of peace with England, the closer he is pushed to the irrevocable first step of his war with Russia."

"So you encouraged him with the most plausible voice that could possibly convey the lie. The voice of a man who happened

to believe it – and happened to be born to the throne of England."

He came back to the corner of his desk and looked down at
me over his half-glasses, tapping the mahogany of the desk with
his finger tips.

"Two fronts. Get him on two fronts. And then, young man,
then . . . You understand?"

He clenched his square fist around the cigar and made quick
short jabs with it.

"You have answered a question for me, sir. I am aware of the
instruction that we are to make no propaganda use of Hess. It's
an instruction people don't understand."

"No. We have neither exulted over his defection nor put him
on display to the public gaze through newsreels and so on. A
fine spectacle: Hitler's deputy, abject, mad and captive. It is
what people expect. Should I do as people expect?"

"Clearly not, sir. Hitler must ask himself why we are making
no public statements; why we are not using Hess for cheap
propaganda. A perfectly good answer is that we are still listening
to what Hess has to say. Perhaps we are arguing behind the
scenes about our response. He knows that you, as the arch
warmonger Churchill, would want to put Hess's head on a
pole. As it isn't on a pole, he may well deduce that there are
powerful voices arguing against you. He may deduce that the
matter is not yet resolved but that you are not in the ascend-
ant."

It was very much the favourite uncle who smiled at me.

"That is an admirably lucid summary. It is my own thinking
entirely. It leaves out only one other, and conclusive reason, for
not putting Hess on display for the maximum possible propaganda advantage."

He stayed silent for some moments.

"And that, sir, is . . ."

"The bugger's dead."

There was a long silence. It was not my place to ask how he
came to be dead. The cigar had finally lost its sweetness and

Winston crushed it in a crystal ashtray. Outside in the park the shadows of the trees were growing long and the mist of new green among the branches glowed in the light of the low sun. Winston stood at the window.

"In public, Hitler says his Deputy has had a brainstorm. But you have noticed that since Herr Hess's arrival the bombing offensive has ended? He has by no means abandoned the idea that Hess's embassy might bear fruit and he is ready either to play from the hand close to his chest or from the dummy. This makes it inconvenient to be without a Hess. We must be seen to have Hess among us. Can we, do you think, make use of your man? Can we pass him off as Hess for practical purposes? He seems to carry off his part very well in your amusing production."

"He seems to, sir. He was filmed entirely alone. The rest of the action was fashioned to suit his behaviour and filmed later. The film you see is a clever blending of the two."

"Extraordinary. You understand what I want? We must keep sustain the idea that Hess is alive in England and in our hands. It has many advantages. Can your man be induced or trained or deceived into serving our turn?"

I thought about it over the glass of brandy. What came back to me was the picture of Uhlsdorf that I'd seen through the Judas hole in the dressing room door: Uhlsdorf, a few minutes away from being the nobody in the fear-damp vest and drawers with his arms wrapped about himself and his cheeks white; Uhlsdorf in the uniform of an officer in the Luftwaffe and standing straight to meet his own reflection and, for the first time, recognising a man of some importance in it.

"I think he might."

"Then, go away. Bring your ideas to me the day after tomorrow. Do not present them to, or discuss them with, anybody else. I need a Hess."

As I was leaving he coughed to detain me a moment at the door.

"I didn't order his head for a pole. He died of a heart attack.

Should there be any breach of security in this matter, however, I will most certainly have your head on a pole."

I did not disbelieve my Prime Minister but, after all, in the course of our conversation Winston had told me that he was sometimes a liar. It didn't make much difference to my job, but I took some trouble to learn the truth. A medical memorandum found its way into my hands, as art dealers say, privately. It was a heart attack. Other things that I learned filled out the picture. Hess had been wounded twice in the Kaiser's War, once very gravely by a bullet passing right through his body piercing a lung. For the rest of his life, continuous exertion left him breathless. He worried about his health. When he parachuted into Scotland, he carried patent medicines in his pockets. He had made a flight of nine hours into enemy territory, ending in a parachute drop, a broken ankle and interrogation. There followed a good deal of being bustled about the country and the shock and humiliation of receiving the treatment due to a criminal, rather than the deputy head of state of the most powerful nation in Europe.

The interrogation was not severe, merely persistent. But as somebody who'd been there said to me, "I think they may have kept him awake rather too long."

We woke him in his cell at about one in the morning and sick dread scraped his face white. I looked down at him and his skin was screaming, while Dieter Maria himself had no other voice.

"Get your shoes on."

The sergeant with me picked up his shoes from the floor and handed them to him. They were prison issue shoes with soft felt soles, made to fall apart if they got wet. He took them as if they were objects of no meaning, put them on the bed beside him and reached for his clothes . . .

"You won't be needing them," said the sergeant, "just get your shoes on."

He sat on the edge of the cot and looked up at me. He had found some voice but it was ragged and choked.

"Warum?"

"Ours not to reason. You must come with us."

We took him from the cell along the silent landing and out of the prison block in his felt shoes and prison pyjamas and wrapped in a blanket.

The squaddie climbed behind the wheel, the sergeant beside him. I sat beside Dieter Maria in the back of the Humber and as the prison gates opened to let us pass out, I pulled the blanket up from around his shoulders and threw it over his head. Nobody in the car spoke until we had gone through Chobham. Then I told the driver to turn up a lane that took us through a wood. He turned off the lane onto a track and finally off the track and onto the leaves under the broad limbs of a stand of beech trees. I removed the blanket from Dieter Maria so that he caught sight of his surroundings in the second before the lights were doused.

We waited in silence. After a while I took out my cigarette case.

"Permission to smoke if you wish to, chaps."

I offered my case to Dieter Maria. He stared at it as a man might stare at a noose.

"Why? I am nobody. I am nobody." He spoke in German. Then he shook his hand impatiently at the cigarette case to wave it away. Like Hess, like me, he didn't smoke. I put the case away.

The sergeant lit a cigarette himself and in the flare of his match I saw Dieter Maria's face. There are men, plenty of them, who are better at doing the sort of thing that I was doing to Dieter Maria. They get better at it because they do it much more often and they enjoy the work. I feel sorry for them.

It was Dieter Maria who first heard the other car arriving. The rest of us paid no attention to it, even when it slid up alongside our own and came to a standstill. The man who got out of the second car was visible only as a slit of dimmed light from his hand torch. We heard the crunching of dry leaves as he crossed to the Humber. The Sergeant wound down the

window and the dimmed torch found his face. The man behind
the torch was still entirely invisible as he spoke.

"I hope you have a puncture outfit."

"Only one for a bicycle I'm afraid," said the sergeant. They
both laughed briefly as if the empty passwords had some faintly
obscene meaning. The voice behind the light had no laughter in
it a moment later.

"We've got him."

The lamp went out and the sergeant turned to the back of
the Humber and said,

"Well, Dieter Maria. It's time for you to make a decision."

The fact that he said it in perfect Munich dialect was what
had the greatest effect on Dieter Maria. His mind went into free-
fall.

"Dieter Maria." I said, "You know that the Stellvertreter
made an heroic flight to England with the Führer's secret
proposals for peace. The English refuse peace. They have
treated the Führer's deputy like a criminal instead of a high
representative of the greatest power in Europe. They have
chosen war. This is regrettable and it is not what the Führer
wanted or expected. He was, however, prepared for it. We
cannot allow the British to hold the Deputy Führer and it is our
job to get him out of Britain. You do not need to know more
about that. Do you find it easy to understand what I am saying
to you?"

Dieter Maria nodded.

"We will take the Stellvertreter to safety. Your job is to take
his place. If the British have their Hess in prison – actually, a
very nice house – our task is easy. If the British are hunting for
their Hess, not so. Do you understand?"

Dieter Maria nodded. I saw him look from me to the
sergeant. We can have been no more than dense shadows to
him.

"You are Kommandoabteilung?"

"That would be the simplest way of saying it. We carry out
the Führer's work."

"But there is now a problem, Dieter Maria," said the sergeant. "Now that you know the truth about Captain James, Captain James is at risk and so are we all."

"No, no. No."

"I'm afraid so. This means that you have a choice. You take the place of the Stellvertreter as we have said or you don't. We have no choice. If you choose not to take on this difficult and important task, then you already know too much. We would have to shoot you."

The Sergeant drew on his cigrette. The glow reflected on the barrel of his revolver."

"But do realise, Dieter Maria," I said, "that should you choose the option of being shot, you would still be helping to carry out the Fuhrer's work and rescue the Stellvertreter. Your remains would be found by the British and it would be apparent to them that a Kommandoabteilung had, regrettably, penetrated British security and assassinated the Stellvertreter. It is obviously not good that the British should hold one who is so close to the mind of the Fuhrer, to be interrogated at will. So you can choose how you wish to serve the Reich: as Rudolph Hess or as some . . . identifiable remains."

The sergeant opened his door and slid out into the drkness. We listened to his footfall on the leafy floor and to the noise, like a distant waterfall, of wind in the leafy roof above us. The sergeant opened the boot, closed it again with a slam and then the door next to Dieter Maria opened to admit, if not light, a less opaque darkness. The sergeant placed a parcel wrapped in brown paper on Dieter Maria's knees. It was just the sort of parcel in which your clothes might come back from a laundry. With quick movements he tore the paper and pulled away the string. These were not the clothes from Berman's Theatrical Costumiers that he had worn before. These were the original articles.

"Either way, you put these on."

A few minutes later we led him, in his Luftwaffe uniform and high fur-lined flying boots to the other car. I opened the back door for him and clicked my heels.

"Herr Hess."

He climbed in and sat next to the other back seat passenger, bulky in the shadow beside him. The sergeant, with the squaddie beside him opened the far door and switched on the internal light of the car.

Dieter Maria turned to see his companion and found that he was looking at himself in death. Rudolph Hess, in a Luftwaffe officer's uniform from Berman's was slumped beside him, his head rolled back on the seat, his mouth open and the eyes under the dense brows so black and cavernous they might have been feasted on by crows.

Dieter Maria looked as if he was screaming but only slight gurgling noises came out of him.

"He is drugged," said the sergeant. With the squaddie's help he folded Hess quickly out of the door and the two of them carried him to the Humber. The noise of his feet dragging through the dry leaves was what stuck in my mind. I've heard it in dreams many times. It had been my idea to show him Hess. It seemed to me that this glimpse of his alter ego made all the rest plausible. I had not quite imagined the moment of standing in the blackness listening to Dieter Maria, sitting in the little pool of pallid light that only made the darkness around him deeper and darker, breathing in the short jerks that come with fear or nausea, and hearing a dead man's feet dragging through the invisible leafmould.

I have no superstitious fear of death or of things that surround death, but it took me a little while to collect myself and get in beside Dieter Maria.

"In your pocket you'll find some photographs. Breast pocket."

He took them out. Pictures of a women. A child. The woman with the child.

"This is your family. You remember them. On the way back, I'm going to give you all the news of them. News from home, Rudi."

In the British Military Hospital, and through the course of his long imprisonment, the prisoner must have been examined by many doctors.

They found themselves treating a Rudolph Hess whose chest and back bore no mark of having been pierced and exited by a bullet that had passed through a lung. This is a trauma that leaves large scars and deformities. The prisoner in Spandau had no such scars. As far as I am aware, only one of the doctors who treated him has commented on this anomaly. Perhaps the others did not call up, or have available to them, the complete medical record of Rudolph Hess. Perhaps the medical record was falsified. That is, after all, quite likely. If so, it was not falsified by me. I did not expect the play to run that long.

Death Duties

It was one of those malicious November days in London when the rain blows right in your face, no matter which way you walk down the street, no matter what way the street faces. Having failed to engage a taxi, I arrived at my club, wet and chilled, to the sympathetic welcome of the porter easing me out of my coat. In discarding the dripping umbrella and curling hat, I discarded also the plans I had made for the day. Two new ones took their place: to put myself outside some hot steak and kidney and a pint of Champagne and, later, to make myself comfortable in the library and write some long overdue letters.

The eating and drinking part of the scheme went through without any problem. Hugo Mainstone joined me, which was enjoyable because he is such a marvellous gossip, but I was glad that he had to go back to Whitehall because I wanted the rest of the afternoon to myself. There was an excellent fire in the library, which made it almost enjoyable to hear the rain lashing at the window. I settled myself with a sheaf of paper and uncapped my pen. Then the steward came in. Mr. Hugh Vaughan had telephoned in the course of the morning. He had asked me to call him back at my earliest convenience. The steward hoped I had seen the message that he had left for me on the board.

I hadn't even looked. I didn't want messages. The steward apologised for drawing my attention to the matter but conveyed that when Mr. Vaughan had telephoned he had laid stress on the anxiety with which he awaited my reply. I hope I am getting across something of the manner of address of the club's senior steward of those days.

I thanked the steward and asked him to bring me the telephone.

All the same, I thought about not replying. Hugh sought and consumed advice the way some men seek and consume strong drink or other gratifications. Giving him advice, which was what his friends did all the time, would have been a more satisfying pastime had he been more inclined to the taking of it. Hugh always found himself in a quandary over any matter large or small. Whenever opportunity knocked, as it did often because he was a lucky and likeable man, Hugh would consult everybody but himself. He would take great pains to get straight in his mind the various arguments for this or that course of action. Then he would do nothing. It was a good thing that he did not depend for his fortune on replying to opportunity when it knocked.

It was not an afternoon for giving advice. Now that I think to mention it, no afternoon is good for giving advice or for taking it. Four o'clock seems to be the sticky patch for the human brain. At four in the afternoon it is so dull as to be negligent of the most obvious dangers; at four in the morning things that are hardly dangers at all grow to be the stuff of despair. Four o'clock is a good time to be asleep, or at least dozing.. The clock said that it was four. The message told me that he was at Gwynant. I knew better, but I called Hugh on the telephone.

"Verdon, it's extremely good of you to call."

"Not at all, Hugh. It occurred to me that you might be looking for a word of guidance on some matter."

The banter was lost on him.

"Could you possibly come down here. Now, I mean. Could you get on a train and come. Please."

"You want me to come to Gwynant? Tonight? But Hugh, it takes forever to get to Gwynant."

"Please, Verdon. I know I'm imposing and I wouldn't ask you, but it is important. I simply do not know what to do. Please Verdon. I'm sure you're the only man who can help . . . or I'm afraid I'm finished."

"Good God, Hugh, what's happened?"

"I can't tell you. Not on the telephone, but it's rather

serious, I'm afraid. It's about as serious as a thing can be. Please Verdon. You're the only man I think I can turn to."

"Hugh, the weather is appalling, I'm rather tired and Plas Gwynant is not at its most seductive in November. It really is out of the question." Rain scourged the window with a sudden rattle of extra viciousness. I said nothing for a while. Hugh didn't, either. I could sense the echoing hall of Plas Gwynant.

"If you could give me some idea . . ."

"If you can't come to Gwynant, then I quite understand. I don't know yet what jail they'll put me in, but I'll let you know and you could perhaps come to see me there."

I didn't say anything. Nor did Hugh. He didn't laugh. He didn't explain the joke.

"Hugh . . . Are you being serious? I believe you are."

"Never more so, Verdon."

"If you'll have somebody meet the next Holyhead boat train, Hugh, I'll be on it."

"Thank you Verdon. I'll meet you myself." He laughed faintly and briefly. "There's nobody else. There are no servants at the Plas any more. I'm the only living soul in the place."

The porter's Bradshaw told me there was just time to finish the letter I was writing, pack a bag and take a cab to Euston. Within the hour I was watching the rain streak along darkening windows as the Holyhead train rattled me to Wales.

The estate of Gwynant lies between the mountains and the sea, inexhaustibly watered by a thousand streams coming down from the wilderness. Looking back from the slopes of Mynydd Goch on a summer's day, its woods and pastures and its haymeadows, billowy with flowers, fill your eye with a prospect of Eden. In the blue distance lie the salt marshes and the wide sands of a great estuary. The picture in my mind is fifty years old, of course, but I doubt if things have changed very much. I'm told that Gwynant is now one of the few places where you can still see a haymeadow with wildflowers. The house, Plas Gwynant, stands on a slight elevation. It might once have been an island, but the sea has long since been called away on other business.

On the Gwynant estate, in its great days, everything was of the estate. If a cottage was built, it was built of bricks fired on the estate, laid with lime that had been burned on the estate. It was roofed with slate from quarries that were the fount of the Gwynant fortune. The produce of the estate was once carried under sail to Liverpool and Bristol from the quays of Porth Gwynant, where today you will find pleasure yachts bobbing on the tide, or beam-ended in the mud. Until not very long ago, whole families lived out their lives without ever travelling beyond his lordship's bounds and without ever eating a mouthful that had not been grown, raised, shot or hooked, netted or snared on his lordship's acres. Gwynant was a world apart, and the last Lord Gwynant of Gwynant was – in a manner of speaking – my friend Hugh Vaughan.

I first got to know Gwynant when Hugh and I were undergraduates and I was sometimes a guest in the vacations. The house, Plas Gwynant, is an enormous jumble of grey stone. Many of the best or worst bits, according to your taste or sense of humour, were tricked up in Gothic by Humphrey Vaughan, the first Baron Gwynant of Gwynant. The second baron was Hugh's uncle David, and the house had been Hugh's home since the age of eight. The entrance hall somewhat resembles the Great Hall of Westminster on a not very much reduced scale. The first Baron's object, apart from overawing his visitors, was to provide space for the display of his trophies, the pursuit of game being the consuming passion of his life. The inclination of the wealthy at that time was to travel the world with a gun, shipping back severed heads. An earlier generation, answering an urge that was not so very different, would have travelled to the Mediterranean with a tutor and sent back pictures and busts. Humphrey Vaughan, being a new aristocrat, followed the fashion of his day with the utmost enthusiasm. He studded his walls with the heads of every kind of animal a gentleman might shoot, each with the date and place of death recorded on a little tablet with the initials of the marksman. Considerable herds of okapi and gazelle from Africa occupied the lower regions. Lions and tigers ranged above them. Higher still were the antlered stag's heads, a colossal moose at the centre. From the hall, high passages led to other chambers and every step of the way you had the company of bestial heads, the trophies, mostly, of more recent Vaughans. At a turn in the westerly passage, the visitor was apt to be startled by the first victim of all this carnage to be preserved in his entirety. A brown bear stood in the corner, hugging a portion of tree trunk and staring with a blistering eye at the door of the billiard room. In that room, as in most rooms of the house, there were smaller and less terrifying examples of the taxidermist's skill. Walls bristled with the masks of foxes and badgers and otters. Somewhere about the house, under glass, in some imposture of its wild surroundings, you'd have found an example of every kind of bird and small mammal to be met with in these islands. Most of these preservations were convincingly morbid but certain of them were vivid and persuasive. In the library was a tableau presenting a hen harrier descending on a stuffed brown hen alarmed for her stuffed little amber chicks, all watched by a quick little stoat. It was bizarre taste, perhaps, but remarkable work. Among the taxidermists who had served the hall, at least one had ranked as something of an artist.

Tanat Evans of Coed y Bwlch was the man with a special gift for taxidermy and he and I were acquainted. The day I met him, Hugh was engaged with some family business or other in Chester and I had gone up to the Llyn to shoot, with Tanat's son Emyr for a guide and companion. A sudden turn in the weather had driven us down the mountain through mist and sleet. Emyr was impervious to rain as to cold. His pace was never hurried but his foot never slipped or took a wrong step and so our pace was rapid. Left to myself, I might have died of exposure. As it was, I was very glad to see the smoke curling from his father's chimney.

Old Tanat evicted his cat from the fireside chair in my

favour and set the black kettle on its hook over the coals and poked up a little blaze. His son stretched his hands towards the fire and called it cheerful, which was as close to an admission of human frailty as I ever knew him to come. There was not much conversation for a while. Gamekeepers are obliged to be suspicious of their fellow men and on pretty bad terms with nature. They set traps and lay poisons. In return, both neighbours and Nature are suspicious of gamekeepers. It means that they are not the most talkative of breeds. Having two generations of them together does not make them any more garrulous. The best way to get to know men like Tanat is to spend a long time not saying very much to them. Emyr left us after our pot of tea to make his rounds. Tanat and I stayed on either side of the fire.

When the kettle burbled again he made another pot of tea, and I remembered that in the pocket of my coat, that hung dripping in the kitchen, was a flask of whiskey. We fortified our cups and as the afternoon settled to an early gloom, so we settled finally into easy talk. The outlines of Tanat's life were simple and clear. He had been born on the estate at Sarn y Bryn. He had been schooled on the estate at Ysgol Gwynant. He had been a gamekeeper on the estate all his life thereafter, starting in the time of the old Lord Gwynant, by which, of course, he meant the first baron who had covered so much wall with trophies. So far as his age and accumulation of small infirmities would allow, he still helped his son in his old line of work. He was at pains to tell me that his cottage and the comforts he enjoyed were everything a man of his age could wish for. All in all, he seemed as perfectly contented as the cat curled up by the fender.

While we were talking of the past he got up and went to his scullery, promising to show me something. He came back with an earthenware bottle, taking dust off it with his sleeve.

"I wonder if this will interest you, Mr. James."

He laid the bottle in my hand, without any suggestion of opening it. I turned it in the firelight and made out the words embossed in a disc on the rough surface.'Gwynant' was spelled out in an arc, and curved underneath,'Gaudeamus'. In the centre of the label was the date 1891.

"Brewed for some special occasion?" I asked.

"Indeed, it was. For the arrival of a son and heir to Gwynant, Mr. James. Celebration ale, it was. Enough was brewed for every man, woman and child on the estate to drink a health; to wet the baby's head as they say. It was a great holiday. Lord Gwynant, you see, had a first wife that could not conceive. He was above the age of fifty before his second wife gave him a son."

"This would have been Hugh's cousin, David?"

"A boy of marvellous promise, Mr. James. I took him up by the Llyn many times, where Emyr has been taking you today. I would say I taught him to shoot, but in truth it was little teaching he needed. If I said he was a man when he was still a boy, would you understand me?"

I looked at the top of the bottle. The stopper was still wired, grimy and stained with rust.

"Did you not . . . wet the baby's head?"

"Very well, indeed. But my sisters and brothers-in-law were teetotal and what was their share, well, I had it. I don't know why, but I had a sentiment to keep a few bottles and not to open them."

In the glow of the fire, the cat stretched himself, licked a paw to draw across his ear, licked it again but seemed to forget what he was about and curled up again to sleep the luxurious sleep of fireside cats for centuries past. I looked at the old bottle.

"Do you suppose it would be drinkable, after more than forty years?"

"I do not suppose so. But it was drinkable after twenty one years. I opened a bottle then. Miraculous, it seemed. That was in nineteen twelve at the coming of age, Mr. James. There was a celebration. A holiday if you like! The school was closed and all the children brought to the house to sing for the family. And sat down after to the biggest feast they ever had seen. Sweet wine, as well, they had, which was not approved of by everybody, but that was his Lordship's whim and I don't see there was harm done. There were races and sports and prizes of money – all the sportsmen of the country were up for competing. A man would run very hard for a chance of ten shillings in those days. Great sports, indeed. A fat ox was roasted at Ty Newydd for David Vaughan at his coming of age and it was not three years before we saw him buried. They brought him back from France and it was said at first his wounds were not too bad, but he died in London in a grand house, I believe, that was turned into a hospital for officers. He had been at a ball, once, in the same house and died in the room where the dancing had been. The body was brought here on a day that was like today and buried at St Mary's on another that was the same. Wicked wet. I opened one of those bottles after the funeral. A sip of it was all I had but it was as good as any beer I ever tasted. A sip was all I took. The rest I poured on the ground, up by the Llyn, where you have been today with Emyr. The year after, the younger brother, Philip, was killed also, but there was no body brought home to bury. And no bottle from his christening to open, of course, but there you are, the first born must have that privilege."

He picked the bottle back out of my hand and took it out to his scullery.

The rain had stopped and, as Emyr had sent word to the house, a trap was sent to take me back. As we drew up the road to Plas Gwynant on its little promontory, the house was no more than a bulky shadow against the last effort of light in the western sky.

At dinner Lord Gwynant turned to me.

"You went up to the Llyn? Not the day for it."

"It wasn't," I said."I had a good soaking and no sport at all."

"Surprised Emyr took you up at all. He sniffs the weather pretty well, usually."

"I may have been difficult to dissuade. We came down pretty smartly, all the same, and dried out at his father's cottage."

"Old Tanat. How is he keeping?"

"Pretty well as far as I could see. But I doubt if he's given to complaining much."

"No. The old sort, Tanat Evans. No complaining."

"Far from it. He was conscious of his good fortune, rather."

"Oh? What was that?"

"The good fortune of enjoying the leisure and dignity of age in a grace and favour cottage at Gwynant. He sang his master's praises."

Lord Gwynant made no reply, other than to stare at me briefly and coldly. He turned and spoke to someone else at the table.

There is a kind of aristocrat who finds the gratitude of lesser men, especially his servants, beneath his notice. Lord Gwynant was not one of them. He cut me dead over it for a far simpler reason. It was no business of mine. I was chastened to be reminded of that.

It was during the night following that dinner that Lord Gwynant suffered the first of the strokes that deprived him of speech and made his last few years pitiful.

I did not stay at Gwynant again before the time that Lord Gwynant died. Had it lain in his power, the title and the estate would have been willed to Hugh but that did not lie in his power and so they passed to Hugh's father. What his uncle could do, he did. Paralysis obliged him to write, when he had recovered that far, with his left hand and with exhausting difficulty. For his last two years, he was almost incapabable of speech. All the same, he managed to write and speak enough to ensure that as much as possible of the cash, with unchallengeable control of the quarries, was left in Hugh's hands and not his father's. Anyone to whom the name of Humphrey Vaughan was familiar would have known why.

Humphrey Vaughan was not among the mourners at the funeral, a lapse that would have been entirely excusable, had the death been sudden, for in those days it took the better part of three weeks to get home from his part of Africa. The day before his liner was due to dock, Hugh called on me.

"I have to go down to meet him, Verdon, I know. But I'd like to have company. Your company if you could spare the time."

"You've seen him, what, twice in twenty years, Hugh? Things have surely changed."

"Yes. I'm not afraid of him any more. I shouldn't think I'll like him any better."

"He may have changed. He may be more pitiable now."

"He may be more contemptible, Verdon. He lives off some unsavoury speculations out there – his women among them. They're not a very agreable crowd he mixes with."

"He's not the worst of them, Hugh."

"No, he doesn't run to the superlative, not even in that."

"Don't bother with hating him. It costs too much."

"He killed my mother, Verdon."

"Her death was an accident, Hugh."

"Her death was his fault."

"But an accident."

"He drove off the road and he did it deliberately because he was drunk and bloody minded and jealous and he didn't care if they both died."

"You can't absolutely know that, Hugh."

"But I do know it Verdon. And I know that he was glad to be rid of her."

"Well ... when he went to Africa and you went to your Uncle, Hugh, you were also glad to be rid of him."

"Yes, I was. I hate to think what a wretched bloody specimen I'd have been, otherwise. Come with me. Get us both through it, Verdon."

We met him at Southampton. Nowadays, the aeroplane conveniently annihilates distance. Ocean liners did not. They used to bring it with them. Humphrey Vaughan peered at the drizzling sky with the eyes of a man who had come a long way.

"Bloody country. Always bloody raining."

I saw Hugh suppress a retort, as if the remark offended him, though it seemed only banter to me.

"I thought you African chaps were always tickled pink to see drizzle and green grass again, Lord Gwynant."

He smiled, more or less.

"Suppose we'd better be. Going to see plenty in Wales."

He and Hugh shook hands. It would have been a brief greeting, but Humphrey Vaughan clamped his son's hand for an extra second or two while he looked over his features.

"Your mother's son, no mistake," he said, letting Hugh's hand drop.

Hugh drove and kept up his silence. I kept up a kind of conversation. The new Lord Gwynant sat in the back of the car occasionally taking a silver flask from the pocket of his coat and drawing privately on its contents. People who'd disembarked from an ocean voyage had a certain smell about them. Part of it was the distinctive bouquet of shipboard laundry mixed with the camphor of long-stored clothes and the leathery musk of suitcases and cabin trunks, all mixed with the one smell made up of a hundred smells, starting with paint and ending with rust, that attaches itself to everything aboard a ship. Part of it was more primal. People who have not lived among us smell different. Neither a woman's scent nor a man's bay rum, with or without other alcohol, can disguise it. The different Lines disembarked passengers bearing subtly different smells. A blind man could have had no difficulty distinguishing between a P & O man just back from India and a passenger of the Cunard Line just ashore from New York. Lord Gwynant smelled of Union Castle, brandy and Africa. I thought it might take more than a a few score head of okapi and gazelle on his walls to make him feel at home.

The scene of his arrival at Gwynant a few days later was described to me in a letter from Hugh.

'You'd have thought it was 1835 rather than 1935. You know that we had a blazing row in London the evening after we fetched him from S'hampton. We had another on the train. Not quite as spectacular but embarassing all the same, and either great fun or a great inconvenience to fellow diners en route to

Holyhead. He was fairly drunk by the time we arrived but I'll
be fair and say he was not incapable. I realise that since he
arrived on these shores I've not seen him when he wasn't drunk
but have never seen him incapable. He had drunk enough when
we had the business meeting with the trustees etc. in London,
but he didn't miss much. He certainly didn't miss the fact
that,my Uncle David had put something of a ditch between him
and most of the cash that didn't go in death duties. Hence
blazing row. Row on train rather more of a personal thing, at
least on the surface, but by the time we arrived you will be in
no doubt as to the state of relations. Imagine, then. A beautiful
day and Porth Gwynant en fete. Bunting and flags in the street.
All the Jubilee stuff out again and children from Ysgol Gwynant
waiting to present flowers and sing songs. I'm only glad that
Jarman fetched us from the station by car and not – as I believe
he'd planned – in the landau. I swear the tenantry would have
unshafted the horses and pulled the pair of us the last mile to
the house. He was better than boorish, to be fair once again,
but not much better. The whole thing embarassed me no end
and I was glad when it was over. Not that it was over before
Stephens presented the household people. He had them lined
up in the hall, starched and scrubbed and dropping curtsies.
Lord G. simply turns to me and says, "where's the money come
from to pay these buggers?" This was not a good start. He is
extrememly agitated about the money. The trouble is that you
can't come to a reasonable agreement with the man. He knows
that the estate will need money. He knows that I have it and
that I am willing to come to an arrangement, but the very idea
of an arrangement sticks in his throat. So he seems to have
decided he'd rather slit his throat than learn to swallow. I tell
him that the money will be there for anything that is a proper
expenditure on the estate. He explodes at this and says I will
only spend money that's going to come back to me. That I'm
only waiting for him to die. That sort of thing. The worst of it
is that there has to be some truth in the charge, but I swear to
you, Verdon, it's not just self-interest. If he could get his hands

on the money, I believe he'd be off to Africa where it would buy him the life of Riley. Mind you, I think by now he's pretty much non grata even in the dark continent. He has, of course, gone through all of his own and all of my mother's money and, obviously, he has debts but he refuses to be candid about them. If we could come to an agreement, I might be able to pay them off. Would this be wise? He complains that Gwynant does not offer the sort of company he likes to keep. I think this has something to do with fornication and Gwynant, as you may imagine, is not quite Africa in this regard so he wants the use of the Chelsea flat. I explained that you have a five year lease that's absolutely unbreakable, so he doesn't care for you, either. I'll find a flat somewhere, but don't worry, you shan't have him for a neighbour. It won't be anywhere nearly as convenient as Cheyne Walk. Better this than have him run up hotel bills that I'm bound to have to pay in the end. It is reasonable that he should have some kind of pied-à-terre and some kind of social life, I suppose, though it's bound to be awkward. I'm preparing for another tussle. Best thing would be if he'd only go back to Africa and some sort of allowance could be made. Would I be the first son to send his father out as a remittance man? You probably know the answer to that. Never mind, though, because I don't think he'll go. He'd rather be back there, all things being equal, but from what I gather they aren't as equal as all that. There's a husband who's promised to shoot him and one or two others ready to take more orthodox (and legal) steps should he show his face. I will see you before the thirteenth. Will you be at Tommy S's? I hope so.

I wrote back and offered to terminate the lease. The reply was a telegram.'Your generous offer gratefully declined.'

It was late and dark when I stepped down from the train. Hugh came striding along the platform with his face turned away from the stinging rain. He grasped my arm and clasped my hand with an urgent strength that said more than any words could have done. "Foul night," was as much as he said. We faced an hour's drive by night through the mountains. The roads were running torrents in places and quantities of rock sluiced down by the water were a frequent obstacle. Though I knew him to be a skilful driver, I thought that Hugh was driving rather too fast in the circumstances and wasn't inclined to distract him with conversation. For his part, he said nothing until we pulled up on the gravel at Plas Gwynant. He switched off the engine and sat back in his seat turning to me.

"Thank you for coming, Verdon. I really do need your advice. The problem is, you see, I've killed my father."

The passage led to the billiard room that I had associated, until that evening anyway, with the hum of after-dinner chat and laughter and fine Havana smoke. Now, the room Hugh led me into was dark and shuttered and the tapping of our footsteps rang a little in the emptiness. Hugh turned on the light and it was starkly clear why he was in need of advice.

Humphrey Vaughan, the third baron Gwynant, was stretched out dead on his own billiard table. You might have said that he was lying in state except that he was wearing pyjamas with a Norfolk jacket. The waxy pallor rather suited his features and it occurred to me that we should arrange for someone to make a death mask. He had been dead long enough for the rigor to have passed and when I turned his head under the light it moved easily, but the weight of it caught the hand by surprise.

"How long?" I asked.

"This morning. About nine o'clock."

The skin was broken and bloody on the left temple. No degree of medical expertise was required to see that his neck was broken.

"And how?"

"He fell from the turn in the stairs."

"That's not quite a whole tale, Hugh."

"We fought and I hit him. He was lashing me with a poker at the time."

"What did you hit him with?"

"Nothing. My hand. I caught him when he was off balance.

Mind, he was off balance from quite early in the day, most days." He looked at the body on the table with despairing eyes. "Why didn't he stay in bloody Africa? Or why didn't he die in Africa? People die of all sorts of bloody things in Africa. Why didn't he? Why didn't he?"

I put my hand on his shoulder and he stopped speaking as if I had covered his mouth. After a few moments he began again, almost matter of factly, as if to give me a summary of details that may have been overlooked.

"He was swiping out with the poker, you see. He meant to do some real harm with it but it wasn't so hard to get it off him. I did and I pushed him away. But then, you see, I had it in my hand. When he came back, trying to grab it again it was so easy just to step aside and hit him with it. I hit him very hard, Verdon. On the back of the neck. I wanted to hit him. I wanted to hit him exactly where I did hit him. And I wanted that poker to kill him. He went over. Over the bannister. Onto the stairs. Went to the bottom. But he was dead before he went over, Verdon. I know he was. I felt the most disgusting satisfaction when the poker hit his neck. Oh, dear Jesus, Verdon! Dear Jesus, I did."

To a reasonably tidy mind it was clear that the events of the day fell into one of three categories: murder, manslaughter or accident. Any decision between the three was the business of the police and the coroner.

"Hugh, why have you called me? You should have called a doctor, the police and a solicitor in that order."

"I know. Yes. But it's the estate, you see. It's the estate."

Leaving Lord Gwynant to silence and darkness on his billiard table, I took Hugh to a small study, lit a fire and descended to the cellar. At most times of anxiety, my advice is to indulge in some small pleasure. On the present occasion I found a bottle of Dow's 1920, decanted it and fetched it up to the study. "I think the principle is pretty much the same as hot sweet tea, Hugh, but it's a good deal more agreeable."

The first glass we sipped and drained in silence. With the second we returned to the only possible subject.

"Was it another row about money?"

"Of course."

"Forgive me, Hugh, but was there a fault on both sides, here? Was it really quite impossible to come to an understanding and make an accomodation with him?"

"Yes. Impossible."

We sipped port. I arranged another log on the fire.

"I said it was about money, Verdon, but it was about much more than money. It was about Gwynant. I think it was his fixed idea to destroy as much of it as he could before he died. My uncle was always a wealthy man, the great man in Gwynant, of course, but a man of some consequence beyond that. The trouble was my father thought he was the more gifted of the two – in some ways, he was – and he resented being the lesser man in the world. But damn it, Verdon, he could have been whatever he wanted to be and he chose to be what he was – and that was a lesser kind of man. In the end he thought life had short-changed him by giving him – far too late – an inheritance that he couldn't quite squander as he pleased. When he started selling things off he claimed he had to, because of the money business. But it wasn't that. It was the lesser man's revenge, Verdon. Undoing what better men have done."

"Perhaps if your uncle had not taken so much trouble to keep things out of his hands, Hugh, it would have turned out differently. He might have risen in his own eyes."

"It would have been a long shot, Verdon. Too much spite in him. You remember when he stepped off the gangway in Southampton, what he said to me? 'Your mother's son, all right,' or something on those lines."

"I remember."

"You know what he meant, I assume? He meant I was my mother's son but not his. After so many years, Verdon, and that's the first thing he chose to say."

"Is it true?"

"You must have heard it mentioned. It's not an especially dark secret."

"I have, Hugh, but in my experience common knowledge often turns out to be a special form of widespread ignorance."

"Well, it's true in this case. My mother loved him quite madly, I think. It made her wretched that she couldn't provide him with a child. He certainly made her wretched about it. In fact, he was a bastard to her about it. So much so that she ended up in somebody else's arms and was somewhat surprised by the result. Me."

"Something of a surprise to him, too, one assumes."

"It had simply not occurred to either of them that the problem might have been his."

"They contemplated divorce?"

"I'm sure they did. The family talked them out of it. Just unthinkable. They were reconciled, more or less. Except that he never was. He couldn't reconcile himself to anything."

Hugh looked at the spot of carmine left in the bottom of his glass and glowing in the firelight. I heard him laugh, briefly and not very loud. It was the sort of laugh you hear from a chess player forced to recognise that he's been check-mated.

"Of course he has his way better dead than alive. Dying is his trump card, really."

"I don't follow you, Hugh."

"Death duties, Verdon. If he wanted to do as much damage as he could to the Gwynant estate then he's doing exactly the right thing by lying there dead. If the estate faces the levy again that's twice in two years. It will mean a lot of breaking up and selling. I inherit, of course, but if I'm about to be hanged . . ." I waved the idea aside.

"No, listen, Verdon. If that were to happen, it would be three lots of death duty in as many years. The estate would be finished. Must I explain why I can't bear that idea?"

"No," I said.

"Some of the tenants would be pleased to buy their farms, of course, but they would be a minority of the people who depend on this estate, Verdon. And it's not just that. It's something you either believe in or you don't. An estate like Gwynant, for good or ill, is a tiny nation. It has its habits and its customs and its loyalties. Dear God, Verdon, it has its dues and its obligations, its myths and legends and its own bloody laws. I found that he'd given notice to a whole raft of tenants. I was appalled. Two days ago, I arrived to find he'd had a blazing fit and sacked everybody in the house."

"All at once?"

"He heard someone, the groom, I think, talking Welsh to one of the other servants and sacked them. He can accept Swahili in Africa but not Welsh in Wales, it seems. Stephens interceded so he sacked Stephens. Mrs. Bowen gave her notice in protest; he told her to get out of the house that instant. The rest of the servants went with her."

"I wonder how long he would have lasted without servants?"

"He couldn't draw water for himself, Verdon. But he insisted he wouldn't take them back. Servants are ten a penny, he said. But he'd been living on what he could scrape out of the larder for two days because he didn't know how to hire somebody. He didn't know who to call and he was too arrogant to ask."

"Do you think he was going mad, Hugh?"

"No. Just perverse. A madman doesn't see what's really going on. He did. The worse it was, the more he liked it. He wouldn't spend money on putting things right about the house and he wouldn't let me spend the money. There are places where the roof is pretty far gone. For want of a hundred pounds now, it'll be thousands in a few years. But he refused to have any work done. I told him the money was there. He refused it. He said I was waiting for him to die. I said he was absolutely right. There was a short discussion of the way I came into the world and he started laying into me with the poker. Does this sort of thing happen in a lot of families?"

"Just as many as you'd think. If the results aren't always fatal, it's mainly luck."

Tears began to flow down Hugh's cheeks. After a while, he sighed and wiped his face with a hand.

"I'm not sure what you think I can do, Hugh."

He looked up at me and though his cheeks were still damp with tears, there was no sign of weeping in his look.

"Oh, I've worked that out, Verdon. I have to die before him."

I looked at him, and I suppose my expression was as blank as my mind.

"If I die before him, I won't inherit, so there'll be no duty to pay on my death, do you see? The title and the estate will go to my cousin Audley. He's only thirteen. There would be time, you see . . . time to recoup . . . And time for me to arrange things so that Gwynant can, with a bit of luck, go on being Gwynant."

"Forgive me, Hugh, but the baron is already dead and you aren't. The order has rather been determined."

"No, Verdon. Look. I killed him. If I were tried, they'd find me guilty . . ."

"That's not a foregone conclusion, Hugh . . ."

"I killed him. They would hang me. Now, what's the point of going through all this business? There's no need for the hangman, I'll do that part myself . . ."

"Hugh . . ."

"No, Verdon. Please listen. I will kill myself. I simply want you to arrange things with certificates and so on so that my death will come first."

"Simply . . .?"

"I'm sure you can do this sort of thing, Verdon. You know all sorts of people. I know you've arranged some . . . some tricky sorts of things for other people. I know you can do it. So much depends on it, and it seems such a small detail to arrange, really. Not that I'm making little of it, Verdon. I know that I'm asking rather a lot."

I sat in silence for some time. When a man has gone a little out of his mind, you save yourself the trouble of reasoning with him. Not that Hugh had lost his reason entirely. His scheme may have been mad and a little fraudulent, but – seen strictly as a method of minimising the tax liabilities – it was quite logical.

While logic is not everything, one had to think the thing out to its conclusion, all the same.

"Hugh, it would hardly be possible to get a doctor to fiddle the certificates. I really wouldn't know how to go about suggesting the idea."

"Can't we keep doctors and all that sort of thing out of it?"

"Not easily. And not at all if you're thinking of doing away with yourself in the very near future. Having two corpses in the same house would certainly give rise to a stewards' inquiry. Who died before whom is a question that would invite the most attentive scrutiny. So I suggest you drop that plan."

"Just . . . just tell me how we can do it, Verdon."

"It needs a little thinking about, Hugh."

The unheated billiard room of a Welsh house in November provides pretty nearly the same conditions as a mortuary, so we had a little time for thinking. Hugh eventually fell asleep in the deep armchair. I covered him with a coat, took the port and a glass and went back to the billiard room to commune with the man at what you might call the still centre of things.

Some may think it odd or unnatural or even, perhaps, perverted in some way to spend a few hours drinking port in the company of a corpse. I'm not going to recommend that you should do so whenever the opportunity might present itself but, all the same, I think you would find it not as disagreeable a way of passing the time as all that. It is not without its rewards. Mere squeamishness over the presence of a corpse is easily overcome. It is no more than a hardly defined superstitious frisson which thousands of very useful citizens have long since forgotten, or they would not be able to do their jobs. Beyond that, you will find that the company of the dead is extremely peaceful. For one thing they do not often interrupt the flow of your thoughts. They are not as entirely free from movement and sound as people are inclined to think, but generally they do not interrupt. Then, too, their presence puts everything into a clear perspective. That, of course, is not the presence of the dead but of death itself.

The light of death is very like the light of the desert, which chisels things to a fine clarity and brings the far mountains very close, without diminishing the sense of space and distance. I have spent a little time in the desert and know why prophets retire into these places. At Gwynant I learned why St. Jerome is always depicted with a skull on the desk of his study.

I think I mentioned that death rather suited Lord Gwynant's features. The skin had always been close to his bones, his eyes always deeply set. If anything, he was handsomer dead than alive by the addition of a certain grave authority that he had never had in life. The lines that an irascible temperament had etched seemed, now they were immobile, to have acquired the air of cold command that Shelley saw carved in pieces of broken statuary. More than faintly, he reminded me of Bellini's Doge, Leonardo Loredan. Ever since that night, in fact, that ruler of Venice has seemed to me to be unmistakably a Welshman. I walked around the table where he lay brightly illumined amid the encircling gloom and imagined him, not in pyjamas and Norfolk jacket, but in the damasked cope and silks of the Doge. Then it occurred to me that the canopied lights of the billiard table were probably rather warm, so I switched them off and left the room in darkness.

Returning to the study where I had left Hugh, I passed once again through the long passage where the walls were studded with the heads of game. Electric lighting was still considered experimental at Plas Gwynant and had not been installed in all rooms, so these heads cast bizarre shadows that swung on the wall as I passed with the lamp in my hand. The shadows on the wall showed a gap where, by the regular pattern, there should have been the head of some quite large beast, its place still marked by the little wooden tablet that belonged to it. The inscription had been painted not long before and so was clear enough to read when I held up the lamp. A buffalo, shot in India ten years or so before, was missing from the herd. Something came back to me.

When I rejoined Hugh in the study, he had woken from

his uncomfortable sleep and was pouring the last of the port.

"Hugh, where is the buffalo?"

"Where is what?"

"The buffalo. Out there in the hall there's a head missing. A buffalo. Where is it?"

"There was something wrong with it."

"What was wrong with it?"

"They hadn't done a very good job or something. The people who stuffed it I mean. Why in heaven do you want to know?"

"Bear with me. Where has it gone?"

"It's been sent to Tanat Evans to see if he can do anything with it."

Tanat Evans. I was pleased to hear that he was still alive.

"Oh he's still alive," said Hugh. "Still in the cottage at Coed y Bwlch."

"And from what you say, he's still capable of work?"

"Hardly. He wasn't sure he could still manage to do anything. He's fit for his age but he's well over eighty. My uncle asked him to try what he could with the buffalo. I suppose he couldn't do much or he'd have brought it back by now. But never mind the buffalo, Verdon. Have you thought . . .?"

"Yes, I've thought, Hugh. And I shall carry on thinking. Get some sleep. I will see you in the morning. But if you slit your throat in the night, I assure you, I'll do nothing at all to alter the clock. So don't even think of it."

The following morning we breakfasted on omelettes and tea. At last, I thought it right to give Hugh an answer.

"I've thought over your idea, Hugh. I think something of the kind would be best and it ought to be arranged."

He reached across the table and gripped my arm in gratitude. In return, I gripped his with force enough to carry my meaning.

"Understand, Hugh, that if we once begin we must go through to the end. If it can be done at all, it can't be done just by the two of us. Other people will have to play a part. I don't know who and I don't know how many, but they will put themselves at some risk. You are the man who must keep his nerve. If you start you must go through with it, whatever it takes."

"Yes."

"And you must be guided by me."

"Yes."

"Then there is no immediate hurry. We are going to have to prepare your uncle for his eventual disappearance."

"Eventual?"

"I thought about this last night in a quiet moment or two with him. It is obvious that he will have to disappear leaving no body to be found."

"I suppose that is obvious, yes."

"He won't be the first Welshman to disappear without trace from his country seat. Arthur Humphreys Owen of Glansevern walked out through the drawing room window one night for a smoke and was never seen again."

"Extraordinary things you know, Verdon. The name is familiar . . ."

"It might well be. Another chap from the same family disappeared just as abruptly – if rather more conclusively – a few years ago. He may have also have decided to go outside for a smoke. He was over the English Channel in an airliner at the time. Whatever was in his mind, he opened the door and stepped outside."

He became very still for a moment then looked up at me with perfect calm.

"And you think that's what I should do?"

"No, Hugh, no. I mentioned that simply because it is of interest, that's all."

He laid down his fork on his plate, wiped his lip with the napkin and put it beside his plate. The condemned man completed a fastidious breakfast, I thought.

"It strikes me as rather a good way to do it," he said.

"But a waste, Hugh. Good God, we'll be at war in a year. There'll be no shortage of the means to die. Lots of people are going to be doing it. It would be much more fitting for you to wait for an occasion when it might do some good. It would better suit the interests of justice, surely."

It was a moment or two before he came to the implication.

"Can we wait that long? What do we do with Lord Gwynant?"

I walked down to the cottage at Coed y Bwlch after breakfast and found Tanat Evans in the little yard beside his cottage feeding his hens. He threw down the food with a trembling movement of his hand but I was glad to see that when he stopped to look at me, as I leaned over his gate, the hand that hovered over the meal in the bowl was calm and still.

"Good morning, Mr. Tanat Evans."

He made no answer for a few moments, then walked cautiously towards the gate.

"My eyes are not so very good without my glasses, sir. Do you object if I look at you close?"

"Not at all," I said, "though you're not missing very much if you don't."

He stopped and the bowl almost slipped from his hand. He caught it up and restrained the meal.

"If I'm not mistaken, it is Mr. James. You are not seeking shelter this morning?"

"No, Evans, I am not. But I may be about to ask you a much greater favour than that. Do you know of a John Price of Newtown?"

"I know a John Price of Fechain and a John Price, Maengwyn, but I have never been to Newtown, Mr. James."

"This particular John Price has been dead a hundred and fifty years or so, Evans. A man that had three wives."

"Oh! Price of Newtown that mummified the wives, the first and then the second, and had them in his house till he married the third. And she would not have them by her and had them buried like Christians."

"You see, I thought with your interests you might know of him."

He leaned on his gate and so did I and we talked a little more about John Price of Newtown who kept his mummified wives beside his bed.

The Welsh gentry, it must be said, had provided ample precedent for most parts of my plan.

While I was in conversation with Tanat, Hugh motored into Porth Gwynant where Stephens was in lodgings, waiting a reply from the agency that would find him another place. It was Hugh's job to tell him that he would not need to look for another place and that things had changed at the Plas. If Stephens was willing to return, his first job would be to find or send word to the other dismissed servants of the house and gather those of them willing to return. That, as things turned out, was not all of them. It was enough.

On my walk back from Tanat Evan's cottage, I called into the little general store in Coed y Bwlch, when my eye was caught by a jar of marbles in the window. I bought a dozen, which I thought would be more than enough for my purpose.

It is not how things are done in murder cases. The murderer had declared himself at the outset. The little cast of dramatis personae called together in the drawing room had, as yet, no notion that a murder had even taken place.

"You will have realised that a serious matter has arisen or you wouldn't be here. It is something that concerns the future of Gwynant. Before we talk about the future, Mr. Hugh has something to say to you."

Hugh stood before the fire. The words he needed were very simple ones, but he could not find them.

"Shall I . . .?" I asked him. After a moment he moved briskly to the door and opened it wide.

"Best, I think, to let everybody see for themselves."

He led the way across the antlered hall and down the passage and past the study to the billiard room. I ushered the company out after him and brought up the rear. I thought someone might have gasped or cried out. No one did. They walked slowly around the table looking at the baron lying in the colourless wintry gloom. They seemed like tourists at a monumental tomb.

"You can see that my father is dead. I want you to know that I killed him," said Hugh, standing at the cue rack.

I held the door open and the little band of sightseers completed its tour of the table and filed out again into the hall and back to the drawing room.

"You are now all aware that Lord Gwynant is dead. The only people in the world so far aware of that fact are in this room. At some time or other, the world must be told but there is nobody whose happiness will be profoundly affected by hearing of it, or whose prospects in life will be altered in any way."

One of the most surprising things about people is how difficult it can be to surprise them. I might have been reading out the minutes of the last meeting of the local history society.

"On the other hand, the interests and the expectations of people in and near to this room are very closely touched by this development. My friend Hugh has put to me a certain proposal which he hopes is in the interest of the estate and everybody on it."

I briefly summarised the liability – the cumulative liabilities – falling on the family under the ordinary provisions of estate tax. Clearly the implications were understood. I looked carefully at each face in turn and saw no note of doubt or incomprehension. What I saw was passive but intense anticipation.

"Mr. Hugh points out to me that it will be greatly to the advantage of the estate if the date of registration of his own death precedes that of his father."

At this a flicker of what Keats might have recognised as wild surmise was visible in the eyes of my listeners.

"Mr. Hugh is determined that he will find a way to atone with his own life for the murder of his father and that should clearly be understood. The alternative way of proceeding is that he should be placed in the hands of the police by any one or more of us in this room and that he should stand trial and be hanged. Were it not for the implications such an outcome has for the estate, I'm sure you know that Mr. Hugh would not hesitate to hand himself over to the authorities straight away. He has asked me to make it clear to you that he is not asking you to choose between your loyalty to those authorities and your loyalty to him. The choice is between the ordinary course of justice and the course of history. The history of Gwynant.

"If you choose the ordinary course of justice, that may well entail the end of the history of Gwynant. That may not mean catastrophe. Who can tell? It may bring improvements we can not imagine. We do not know who will buy what part of the estate, who will buy what farm, or wood, or moor, or who may buy this house should it be auctioned. You may take the view – I would be wrong to try to persuade you otherwise – that no law of nature says that it is right for a Vaughan and only a Vaughan of Gwynant to have the stewardship of these things. The fact that it has been so for a long time is not, of itself, much of an argument. To many minds that might be an argument for change. Mr. Hugh's conduct and his uncle's conduct before him are the only persuasive arguments known to me that I can put before you. You know better – much better – than I do what those arguments are worth. You don't need me to turn them into words. What can I say to you? You will not find the reason for your choice in my words but in your own hearts when you consider the future of Gwynant. Remember, no one is asking you to choose whether Mr. Hugh will die or not die. The choice is rather, shall he die now and, perhaps, Gwynant with him; or shall he die later and bequeathe whatever he can of Gwynant to posterity?"

I looked about the room in silence, and all of them looked back at me, in silence. I saw Jarman, standing below a lamp, his hollow cheeks in deep shadows; Mrs. Bowen seated on the Louis Quatorze she had been almost superstitiously afraid to take her place on and of which she was now entirely oblivious; Owen, the general man, whose nearly crimson features had paled almost to pink and whose habit of nervously clearing his throat had, for once, fallen into complete abeyance. Stephens, short, plump and composed stood with his hands one upon the other on the back of a chair. He might have been waiting for a sign to bring in the soup. Sometimes they looked at me and sometimes at Hugh, but no one spoke.

"It would hardly be right to ask you to argue this matter out aloud with me or each other and certainly not with Mr. Hugh. And yet, either we all agree on the one course, or it must be the other. If even one of us believes that it would be wrong to postpone justice, then Mr. Hugh will call the police tonight. A public show of hands can hardly be the way to decide, but we must know whether we are unanimous, or not."

I picked up a bag that I had put on the table in front of me. Under it on the inlaid pattern stood seven black chessmen. The bag was the sort of thing we used in those days to put shoes in when travelling. Nowadays, I use the plastic things one gets from supermarkets but in those days a shoe bag was made of stout cotton with a drawstring. From my pocket I took a handful of marbles.

"There is a way for us all to state our decision in a secret ballot. I am putting in this bag a marble for each one of us in this room." The seven marbles clicked into the bottom of the bag. From the table I took the seven black pawns.

"And with them, a pawn for each of us. I'm going to ask each of you to take from the bag one or the other, a pawn or a marble. If you feel that you can square it with your conscience to postpone justice, take out a pawn. You will feel the shape. Don't look at it and don't allow any of the rest of us to see what your choice is."

I went round them one by one with the bag. One by one they took whatever they chose. I went back to the table where I had placed a large ashtray and with no ceremony at all emptied the bag. The glass marbles chattered and bounced on the crystal. Six of them. And one pawn.

When the sound of the marbles in the ashtray ceased the silence was profound. It was broken by the scraping of Hugh's chair.

"Thank you, all of you. It's good to have a decision. I have a telephone call to make."

Hugh walked from the room and crossed to the study.

In the drawing room no one moved. They seemed transfixed and it was hard to know how to bring their part in things to a close. Rather oddly, I heard myself saying, "There is no further business to attend to, thank you all very much."

Then Emyr walked forward from the back of the room to the the table in front of me. He picked out the pawn and clenched it in his hand. Then he took the marble from his pocket and dropped it among the others.

"Don't tell him it was me, Mr. James. But I wanted to know if he would."

"No, Emyr, you've changed your mind, that's all. But the ballot was final."

He hesitated, staring at the marbles.

"Emyr, he'll be very grateful to you. You have taken an enormous burden off his shoulders. It is by far the easier way for him."

Emyr ran from the room. Through the open door of the study he could see Hugh at the telephone. I saw Emyr cross the hall in very few strides and put himself in front of Hugh. He opened his clenched fist to show him the pawn. I saw Hugh's face. Though it was turned only a little toward me, I could read it easily and I read dismay. A man who thought he had been excused a terrible duty had found himself in Gethsemane after all.

There were two objects, as I saw it, in preserving Lord Gwynant. The first was to avoid the dangers that attended immediate disposal of the corpse. A body buried may be dug up, a body discharged overboard from a small boat may be brought up in a trawl or washed ashore. Burning a body requires, as anyone who has been down to the Ganges at Benares will know, a good deal of fuel and a conspicuous blaze. The process makes itself conspicuous in other ways as well. This sort of thing is best not done in haste or while in a state of distress. The friends who arranged the cremation of the poet Shelley on an Italian beach thought the idea fitting and romantic before they put the torch to the kindling. Their accounts tell us that they regretted the notion shortly afterwards.

While we could hardly give Lord Gwynant a funeral with plumed horses, I had a deep objection, as did Hugh, to the idea of mere disposal. It would not have been right to abbreviate the obsequies to a secret indecency. In time, and after the reflection that time would allow, it would be for me to arrange the matter in some fit way. Until then he could have been kept as an embalmed corpse in his own cellar, awaiting a very private funeral at the right time. That, however, would not quite have met our needs.

The corollary of the fact that Lord Gwynant had to disappear was that it was necessary for him to appear, or be capable of appearing, until shortly before the date of his disappearance. Then the seven years would begin to run until the legal presumption of his death. This was the second object of his preservation. To remove all trace of Lord Gwynant immediately would entail a risk that the clock would begin to run too soon, should somebody begin to make enquiries about him. Lord Gwynant should be seen occasionally about the place. An unsociable man like Humphrey Vaughan was not necessarily seen about very frequently, but even a recluse or an invalid would be seen from time to time. His passing through the town in a motor car would be remarked now and again, at the very least. So, in addition to the simple business of preservation by embalming, a degree of taxidermy was also required so that the world might, occasionally, catch a glimpse of him, and see some lifelike flash of his old self.

I had explained what was necessary to Tanat Evans and suggested that I might help him as an extra pair of hands. To my vast relief, he declined my offer. Emyr would be his only assistant. It was a good thing that Plas Gwynant had been brought thoroughly up to date in respect of plumbing and running water, which was not always the case in country houses in the nineteen thirties. I supplied them with formaldehyde and a number of scalpels. Horsehair, iron wire and other small necessities Tanat supplied from his own stock. They worked in the principal bathroom while Hugh and I waited, mostly in silence, in the drawing room. It was the earliest in the day that I have ever pulled the stopper from the Scotch indoors, though I've enjoyed the stuff for breakfast when stalking deer. I had no idea at the start of the day how long the business might take and I hadn't asked. I imagined that for all his experience with beasts and birds, even Tanat had no way of knowing. In the end the job took fourteen hours.

When they came down to the drawing room, it was long after dark, and the lamps were lit. Each of them accepted a glass of whiskey with a hand that was, I confess, steadier than mine. I was conscious that they had not eaten all day, but Tanat dismissed the matter.

"There will be plenty of time for eating, Mr. James. Anyway, you do not get hungry when you are consumed in what you are doing."

"I had no notion that it would take so long, Evans. You've certainly kept at it."

"It would have been quicker but for the neck being broken, Mr. James. That had to be put right, of course, and the wire I had thought to use, well, it wasn't strong enough. It is very heavy, the head, and the wire I was using was bending, but we got it right in the end."

Hugh was looking pale and I took the trouble to refill his glass.

"We doubled and trebled the wire on itself, you see, and the advantage is the head is able to be adjusted a little. If you are ready, sir, to take a look? I hope you will think it all you were expecting."

It was very much more.

They had adjusted the head with a pensive inclination, slightly sideways and drooping towards the collar bone. Tanat had been right about the glass eyes. Even with formaldehyde, he had insisted, the originals would seem unnatural. The pupils were the problem. They either open up entirely or close tight, I can't remember which. Getting hold of the glass eyes had presented a slight difficulty. A singleton is the usual order. The customer requiring a matching pair will be the subject of curiosity. I was obliged to impersonate the proprietor of a seaside waxworks when making out the order and there was some delay in filling it. Lord Gwynant had been obliged to wait several days in his wine cellar, wrapped in oil cloth and packed in ice.

Tanat had done well with the eyes. At one moment, while Hugh and I were pacing about the drawing room, it had occurred to me to go up to the scene of the operation and say that he must on no account give Lord Gwynant the sort of glare that made such an impression on everyone who saw the brown bear opposite the billiard room door. It was not difficult to resist the impulse to interrupt the two men but the possibility had troubled me again as we made our way to the bathroom. My fears had been groundless. I should not have forgotten that Tanat Evans was the Cellini of taxidermists. Lord Gwynant's expression turned out to be not at all like the bear's. He sat in the wheelchair that his brother had been brought to by strokes, his head supported by his left hand, all but the index finger folded under his cheek bone. His gaze was deflected downwards, as if he were reading something on his knee, or perhaps reflecting on something he had just read there. There seemed a pregnant possibility that he would look up the moment he became aware that you were in the room.

I commented on the very natural composure of the muscles of the face and the convincing and recognisable expression they created.

"It was the setting of the expression that took the time, Mr. James. Anybody could do the job and have him look half mad or stark terrified but it's not what you want."

"No," I said.

Both men stood back in silence to gaze at his lordship.

"It's the best you've ever done, Da. I'll say that," said Emyr.

*

It was no special prescience of mine to know that war was around the corner. Anyone with common sense knew that and by nineteen thirty eight there was enough common sense about for the government to start printing the ration books. The ration book business comes to mind because, of course, Lord Gwynant was issued with his ration book in the course of time. If I remember rightly, some kind of emergency census was conducted soon after war broke out and Stephens quite naturally included Lord Gwynant among the inhabitants of Plas Gwynant. In due course, the ration book arrived.

A meeting of the household, whom I now thought of as The trustees, decided that the extra should be given from time to time to local families whose fathers were on active service or in the merchant marine. When even a smallholding, let alone an estate like Gwynant, could feed its people perfectly well, rationing or no, this could hardly have involved a very great sacrifice, not even had Lord Gwynant had been blessed with a heartier appetite. All the same, in the harbour cottages of Porth Gwynant, it was a token very well received. Indeed, I believe it may have caused the first flicker of public affection for the new Lord Gwynant.

At the time, Hugh was in France with the Expeditionary force.

Chapelle D'ou. May?
Verdon, my old friend.
Something of a brief lull here, not that I understand why. As far as I can see, there's no reason Jerry shouldn't just keep coming, roll us up and spit us out. I hope it doesn't mean that somebody, somewhere is talking about surrender. I'm giving this to someone who may get back sooner than I, though how this shambles can hope to be embarked, I can't see. Anyway, I hope this gets to you.

Some of us are going to have to stay here, dig in and hold them up as long as we can. Ils ne passeront pas. Except that ils passeront, of course. No two ways about it. But we'll have done our bit. I very much hope that I'll have done mine, and that you will think I've discharged my obligations.

This letter was written in the first hours of daylight and reached me on the evening of the same day. It was the day we pulled back two squadrons of fighters from the lost cause. The men they left on the ground had long days of a slogging match to bear. Many of them were at last embarked only to be blown out of the water. The Hurricanes were at Biggin Hill in less than twenty minutes. The pilot of one of them had Hugh's letter tucked under his Mae West.

As we sat in the smoking room at my club, the Flight Lieutenant was not in an especially ebullient mood. Not many people were, so there was no need to excuse the long silence into which the letter threw me. After a while my messenger drained the last of his whiskey and looked around him.

"Dead and alive sort of hole. Why don't we go to a pub and get drunk?"

"You should get drunk, by all means," I said, "but I don't think you should get drunk with me."

"Why not?"

"You should get drunk with people of your own sort."

"What the hell does that mean, Verdon?"

"You should drink with heroes, I should drink with clerks."

"Oh come on, Verdon. You've pestered everybody to get into some kind of show. Everybody knows that."

"And some of them say you can afford to be importunate when you know perfectly well you'll be turned down. Thanks for your trouble, Paddy, but I won't join you. And you'll have a better time if I don't."

I said goodbye to him on the steps of the club. When he was four months older, Paddy Synge was to be widely known as a hero. He would never be five months older. If I felt some foreshadowing of that as I watched him walk towards Piccadilly, it wasn't clairvoyance. It was how things were. I put Hugh's letter in an inside pocket and did what Paddy was going to do. I went to a pub and set myself steadily to the task of getting drunk, but I did it alone. Until the time came when I couldn't think straight at all, I thought about Hugh and about what I had to do at Gwynant.

Except that I didn't have to do it. In front of me today is a copy of the citation for the award of the MC to Lieutenant Hugh Vaughan.

"Realising the imperative need for immediate action, and unable to communicate with his men or his commanding officer, Lieutenant Vaughan, with entire disregard for his own chances of survival, attacked the Panzer whose fire was preventing their withdrawal. Without any covering fire, Lieutenant Vaughan crossed fifty yards of open ground to take up a position from which he was able to bring fire to bear on the driver of the tank who was operating with his clear vision panel open. This was an exceptional feat of marksmanship.

Climbing aboard the tank, Lieutenant Vaughan disabled it further with a grenade attack via a damaged engine ventilator. During this attack, Lieutenant Vaughan came under fire from a German position fifty yards away. His commanding officer, now relieved by Lieutenant Vaughan's action, was able to bring a machine gun to bear and suppress the enemy fire.

The crew of the Panzer surrendered to Lieutenant Vaughan, but the prisoners were abandoned as Lieutenant Vaughan's company continued its withdrawal."

There were plenty of people who thought the award should have been the VC. Some observed that it probably would have been had Lieutenant Vaughan – now Captain Vaughan, of course – been available to be ballyhooed a bit in the cause of public morale. He was not available, of course. He had been taken prisoner later the same day having stayed behind to cover the withdrawal of his company to an embarkation point. The Red Cross report said that he had received excellent treatment for his wounds and that he was recovering well. A footnote to the report said that Lieutenant Vaughan was much admired by his captors and was embarassed to be the object of privileged treatment on this account.

When this report reached England, I was obliged to send a telegram to Stephens cancelling certain preparatory arrangements that we had made that would have led, in their turn, to the cancelling of Lord Gwynant's ration book. It began to look as if Lord Gwynant would be distributing his points and coupons to the needy for some time.

It was a long time before I received a letter from Hugh through the Red Cross.

Dear Verdon,

I want to say how grateful I am that you agreed to help me. Glad in a particular way that I didn't foresee. I hope and believe that it justifies everything that we did. It's true, as you said, that if we'd gone about it another way, there would have been one less chap available to do his bit. But I don't make the mistake of thinking my bit has been all that important. Hard to have any such illusion in these times. The important thing that I want you to understand is that, the other way, I'd never have come to forgive the old man. Never have had a chance to, perhaps. To understand all is to forgive all. You will recall which particular Frenchman said that. I'm afraid I don't have any works of reference to hand. Did he observe that you can also start by forgiving and find that you then begin to understand? It's a more practical way round, too. Not such a tall order. If you have to start off understanding all, not much forgiving will get done. I'm glad I was given the chance.

Funny isn't it to be glad of having seen so many rather bloody things. But there we are, it alters perspectives. I thought him a great monster once, but he seems a very small one now, and really no monster at all. Are some people just not capable of happiness? Giving it or receiving it or knowing what it is? A deformity, but not monstrous. I couldn't see that until I had become monstrous myself.

I am acutely aware that you are left in a potentially embarassing position and it must be time to unburden yourself of any obligation towards me.

Again, many thanks. Your friend,

Hugh Vaughan.

I wrote back to him, via the Red Cross.

Dear Hugh,

It is good to hear that you are well and especially good to know that you are on much better terms with your father. It pleases me very much to hear that. I have had a meeting with the trustees and they have resolved – nem con – to maintain the status quo. There are no developments that need concern you. Your father's health continues much as ever, but he was recently well enough to attend a concert in Porth Gwynant in aid of the Spifire Fund. Unfortunately he had to leave early and was not able to address the company, but he gave every indication of enjoying the music. I have spoken to Stephens about this, wondering if these outings were altogether wise, but he assures me that they are not hazardous to his Lordship and the community is always glad to see his Lordship out and about. He is really quite a popular man down there now, as he gives his rations to people who might otherwise go very short. The needs of everybody at the Plas, of course, are met abundantly by the garden and the game alone. Not to mention the cellar. All is well. Try to keep your spirits up.

Ever yours,

Verdon.

It was in nineteen forty three that they made their escape from the camp. Out of a dozen, two were shot and seven recaptured inside twelve hours. Hugh and the two Australians, Robertson and McIntyre, reached Spain after weeks of extraordinary dangers and privations and with the help of many brave men and women. I could not do justice to that story. An account of it is to be found in Alan McIntyre's book, Thorn In Their Side. Robertson, of course, was lost when the ship bringing him from

Portugal was torpedoed in the Western Approaches. McIntyre and Hugh reached England, collected their back pay and returned to soldiering.

He walked into the club in a Captain's uniform so new it looked as if it might have stood up on its own.

"Fits me like a pair of curtains, I know," he said, "but by the time I get used to the pips, I intend to have put a bit of weight back on."

"I'll buy you the best dinner in town just to get the ball rolling. What are you drinking?"

"Nothing. Just water. Had a touch of hepatitis sometime."

He did not look remotely jaundiced. He was thin and his face was quite different. It was Hugh's face but pared and heavily engraved. I had expected him to be pale, because one thinks of prisoners as pale, but he was as weatherworn as a shepherd.

"You must get up to Gwynant if you want to fatten up. How much leave have they given you?"

"Nobody wants to see me for two weeks. And yes, I must get up to Gwynant."

His tone was negligent. It suggested that getting up to Gwynant might be a social duty he was in danger of overlooking.

There was about him an enveloping air of not belonging. Just as his body did not belong inside the crisp uniform, so the worn face was out of place among the sleek and comfortable furnishings and sleekly comfortable clubmen. The steady blue eyes that turned to me did not belong to the Hugh that I had known.

Here was the gaze of a man you might catch sight of through the window of a train; a man who has stopped at some place that happens not to be his destination.

"Sorry," he said at last. "I know we ought to talk about Gwynant."

"Oh, you'll find things pretty much as they were. You got my letters?"

"Allowing for the censor's habit of taking out sentences at random, yes, I got them. Thank you. I didn't quite understand. My father seems to have recovered enough to go out to concerts. Is that right?"

"Not often, Hugh. On occasions when his position really demands it. Noblesse oblige. You understand."

"No," he said. "Not sure I do."

"Well, like you I was surprised and . . . alarmed to hear that he'd been out and about. But Stephens tells me his outings have been very carefully supervised. They try to spare him the trouble of having to be sociable and that sort of thing."

"I hope they succeed."

In my wallet I had a clipping from the Cambrian Post and Echo.

"Stephens sent me this. You might care to see it."

Musical Feast At Porth Gwynant,

"Music by Handel was among the splendid offerings at a Noson Lawen given at Porth Gwynant Grammar School by the Gwynant Choral Society last Saturday. The Society's patron, Lord Gwynant, who is confined to a wheelchair by ill-health resulting from his many years in Africa, attended the concert. Although his Lordship was obliged to leave before the national anthem was played, he made it known that he was delighted by the proceedings and paid the Society the compliment of saying that their performance was 'up to the highest professional standards.' Commenting on the fact that the composer Handel was a German by birth, Mr. Rhodri Evans pointed out that he had lived and worked in London and would have surely have been pleased that his music should help to raise money for the Spitfire Fund to defend the city he loved. George Handel is not the only German the Society has plans to enlist. Mozart, Bach and Beethoven will all be contributing to their concerts in the coming season, said Mr. Evans.'

"I gather from Stephens that Lord Gwynant not only left early, he also arrived a little late, but our reporter is too polite to mention it."

"Why? I mean why did he go at all?"

"Because, Hugh, in these times it seems there's a limit to the number of patriotic events you can decline to attend."

"But he's . . . extremely ill. Surely people understand?"

"Not too ill, some local people have said, to go taking motor trips, using up precious rationed petrol. I'm afraid it was my idea that he should occasionally be seen abroad in the Daimler."

"I still don't see . . ."

"I think they were right, Hugh. There are rumours, you know, that certain people in Wales are disaffected. It is said that German bombers have been guided in to their raids on Liverpool by radio transmissions from Wales."

"Good God! There can't be any truth in it."

"I daresay not, Hugh, but rumours are one part of our diet that isn't rationed. As I say, I suggested the motor outings, and it was also my idea that he should usually take these trips in the evening as darkness was beginning to fall. When the rumours about the radio signals began to circulate, somebody added to them by wondering where it was that his Lordship went. They'd worked out that he didn't call on anybody. Somebody seems to have thought a Daimler would be big enough to conceal a radio as powerful as you like. A few people seem to have remembered that before he went to Africa, he had more than a little regard for the Nazis. It seems he once said that "this country needs either Moseley or Mussolini in charge and I don't much mind which.""

"He certainly didn't say it at Gwynant. He was hardly ever there."

"He was quoted in a national paper. They remember these things up in your misty hills."

"You seem very well up on the gossip at Gwynant."

"Stephens keeps me abreast. He also told me that his Lordship decided to make it clear that he was right behind the war."

"Stephens should do as you tell him, Verdon."

"I can't always be available, Hugh. We should be very

grateful to Stephens. He has a cool head. We should be very glad that he also has fallen arches and the services won't take him. Anyway, I don't think your father will be making too many trips in the future."

He didn't say anything. For some time he looked at the far wall of the smoking room with his man-on-a-train eyes, then suddenly he looked back at me and I saw for a moment the old Hugh.

"It wasn't supposed to go on this long."

"Nobody ever said how long, Hugh."

"It should have been a matter of hours. Minutes, even. That's all. A little adjustment. How did we get here? How did we come so far on this road?"

"By taking the first step along it, Hugh."

"I can't remember why, any more. Well, I can remember, I just can't remember why it was important."

"It was to preserve something, Hugh. And the reason for preserving things is just that: that the best of us will sometimes forget that they are worth preserving."

He was silent for a while again, and the man-on-a-train look returned to his eyes.

"I can't go up to Gwynant, Verdon. I'm sorry, but I can't."

"It will be expected, Hugh."

"That's why I can't go. For one thing they'd treat me as a hero which is a degree of deception I can't altogether stoop to."

"It wouldn't be a deception."

"It would, Verdon. I'm not a hero and if you want proof I'm giving it to you: I'm not going to Gwynant. I'm not going because I haven't got the stomach for it. I'm funking it. I wake up in the night with the sweats. I know that I never will go there again."

"Then let's not discuss it further. I'll tell you what, why don't we go to a play? Then we could meet some people for a little supper and go on."

"Will we get tickets for anything good?"

"Oh yes. I can get tickets."

"I suppose you know somebody?"

"As it happens."

"I should have remembered. You know everybody."

"I wouldn't say that. I seem to have bumped into some actors lately, that's all. Would you care for it? A play, I mean."

"Well, a man who can't drink during the evening needs something to take his mind off it. A play sounds splendid."

The play was entirely forgettable which was exactly what the audience wanted. We had a thoroughly good time clapping at the end of it. Diana, especially, had been bright and winning, rather outshining the leads, I thought.

As we made our way out of the theatre the conversation around us had the pleasant fizz that you hear when people feel they've had a jolly good night of it.

"What did you think of Diana Fanshawe?"

"Which one was she?"

"She played the younger sister. The one with the shocking secret."

"Oh, I thought she was marvellous."

"Good, because you're going to meet her. If you can't drink, you'd better be introduced to some other intoxicants."

There was a crush backstage and I almost regretted bringing Hugh along. With his weatherbeaten face and wearing what seemed to be somebody else's uniform, he seemed more out of place than ever. Perhaps, even worse, he might not have been thought out of place at all but taken for an extra. A spear-carrier. In a welter of people taking an extraordinary amount of notice of each other, no one, I thought, took much notice of Hugh. I was wrong it seemed.

"Who is your friend?" asked Diana on the way to the Lapin, "and hasn't he got the most gorgeous sad eyes?"

"His name's Hugh, I've known him since Oxford and, yes, I suppose he has."

It was a large party by the time we arrived at the Lapin, and we took up most of the rear room. It was Dorian who patted the chair next him and drew Hugh to what, in another world, would have been the High Table.

"I've got your rank, old chap, but I don't think anyone's given me your name and number. I'm Dorian Lisle."

"Dear me," said Hugh. "So you are. I didn't realise the moustache wasn't real. Hugh Vaughan. I enjoyed the play very much."

"As long as you were completely taken in by the moustache, dear boy, then my life and training have not been in vain. God bless you for your kind words."

Dorian turned to the rest of the company while breaking a bread roll in an entirely absent-minded way that had all the gravity of priesthood about it and spoke effortlessly above the chatter.

"Captain Vaughan is kind enough to tell me that he thinks my moustache is an absolute triumph. I shall certainly keep it."

"The play may close but the moustache will run and run," said somebody.

Dorian turned back to Hugh.

"Well, you know what we've been doing. What have you been up to, Hugh my dear?"

In his present state I was unsure how receptive Hugh might be to Dorian's bravura style of conversation. I need not have worried. I saw him smile for the first time in the day.

"Nothing nearly so entertaining, I'm afraid. In fact I've been doing remarkably little for the last two years."

"I thought to look at you you might have been out in the desert."

"'Fraid not."

"You've been doing something admirable or you wouldn't have that ribbon for me to admire. That's something rather gallant, isn't it?"

"Rather a long time ago and it's not nearly as convincing as your moustache. Let's not talk about it."

I knew that Hugh would rather not have spoken about himself at all, and that he would certainly not want me to tell the company why he had been decorated. On the other hand, as the object of Dorian's interest he had become the object of everybody's interest.

"When Hugh says he hasn't done much for a couple of years, Dorian, he may be right. It depends whether you think escaping from a prisoner-of-war camp counts as much."

It brought the attention of the pair of tables.

"Oh, well done," said somebody.

"I know you. You're the chap I've read about. You were all over the papers," said Hermione Street.

"Were they kind to you, darling? They've been beastly to me." asked somebody, to be rewarded with a modest bouquet of laughter.

"We are in the company of an authentic hero," said Dorian Lisle. "Now as you know, I am shortly to play an authentic hero myself, so talk among yourselves while I hog Captain Vaughan and get some tips."

I would not have believed that egocentricity could have been put to such tactful use, but I knew that Dorian had seen Hugh's discomfort and had eased him off the hook of attention. The actor turned to him and offered the bottle of wine.

"I've been told not to for a couple of years," said Hugh.

"Wartime years count double," said Dorian. "When did they tell you that?"

"About a year ago."

"Well there you are."

"It was something of a joke at the time. Not much Chablis about."

"There is now."

Hugh smiled and pushed his glass forward.

It's not that actors are like children: actors are children. They are children who have that best of all costumes in the dressing-up box, a real grown-up body to play in. To grow up is, for most people, to reach the state of being embarassed by make-believe. Being very grown-up amounts to moving on from embarassment to contempt. But the fact is, of course, that most of the grown-ups are really involved in make-believe all the time without recognising what they are doing. At least the actors know. It makes their company agreeable to me. That evening at The Lapin, I could see that it was agreeable to Hugh as well, and the more pleasurable because it was a novelty. He felt himself to be a bogus hero; perhaps it was therapeutic to be in the company of men and women who were bogus heroes and heroines by profession.

Really we were at a splendid children's party, except the food was far better and the children, as I say, had proper grown-up bodies to play in and Hermione Street was famous for having one of the most perfectly grown-up bodies in England. Her most famous features, made striking in every picture that one ever saw of her, were her shoulders.

"It was an absurdity, darling. They had swaddled, absolutely swaddled, me to the ears. I was carrying so much cloth over my shoulder, I might have been playing Rob Roy. I told them to remove about a yard and a half. So the silly creatures turned up with the most outrageous décolleté thing you have ever seen. Brigadoon one minute, The Windmill next. I should certainly have needed the largest possible fan. 'That is what we thought you meant,' they said. Decency, darlings, I said. Decency. I simply want some air about my salt cellars and then I can act."

"That is an absolute necessity is it?" I asked, my tongue a little in my cheek.

"Of course it is, Verdon, darling. Acting is entirely to do with the shoulders and nothing else."

I laughed.

"Not even the voice?" I asked. "Surely the voice plays some part?"

"I assure you, darling, that if you listen to me you'll find I say everything in a perfect flat monotone. Nobody notices. I put all the meaning in with my shoulders."

We all laughed dutifully, but she wagged a finger as if we were being impious.

"I absolutely mean it. Acting is like shooting. If you want to hit them between the eyes, it has to come straight from the shoulder. If you've got shoulders, you can do anything. Shoulders and cheekbones."

She reached up to the shaded lamp on the wall behind her and cocked its shade to one side so that the light glared down at her.

"Garbo," she said. And suddenly her head was lying on her shoulder as if offering her pale throat to be either kissed or slit. One hand dragged her hair straight down her cheek and she spoke in her perfect monotone.

"My darling you have made me know what it is to be a woman."

There was something in her claim that she knew how to make her shoulders eloquent. The only inflection she gave to the line was a kind of surrender of her shoulders. It was rivetingly sensual. There was applause and a good deal of laughter but she ignored it. She turned her other profile to the light, took a cigarette from somebody's lips and said,

"Dietrich."

And in a little skein of cigarette smoke, with shadows under her cheekbones, there was Marlene Dietrich. With the tip of one finger, she flattened her nose and spoke in her perfect monotone.

"Mein liebchen, you have made me know what it is to be a woman."

Her shoulder moved. I cannot describe how – the attempt would be ludicrous – but its movement was laden with irony and amusement. The company howled with laughter. She returned the cigarette and took up her drink again, smiling. For a few moments the smile fell on Hugh. Dorian turned to me, laughing delightedly as he spoke though he had seen the display many times.

"You know, do you, that in Account Rendered she had to sing? She can't sing a note of course . . ."

"I can," said Hermione, "but nobody can ever make out what note it is!"

"And you know what The Times said? 'It hardly mattered that Miss Street cannot carry a tune. She fluttered her collar bones in a musical way and the audience adored her.' And they did."

Some time later, I turned from talking to somebody else and

saw that Hermione's shoulders were in what might have been called their melting mood, and were generously turned in Hugh's direction.

"What was it you dreamed of most frequently? When you were in your prisoner of war camp?"

We had reached the brandy by this time and people had got up and moved about the tables. Other people had joined us and one or two had left. There was an empty chair now between Hermione and Hugh, and she leaned with one arm along the back of it to ask him her question.

Hugh smiled back a little blankly, as if surprised to be spoken to. One glass of wine has its effect on a man who has drunk nothing for a year.

"What did you see in your dreams? Hearth and home? Family? Old friends? Green fields?"

"All of those."

"What blameless dreams you heroes have."

"No. All my dreams are nightmares."

Hermione Street laughed and then inclined her head, widening her eyes.

"Do you mean that?"

He looked at her without saying anything.

"Did you not dream of lovers?"

"None to dream of."

"I find that hard to believe."

"Well, it's true," said Hugh.

"You must have loved somebody once. At least once." She looked at him with disconcertingly open eyes. "Was it a boy or a girl?"

Hugh laughed a delighted laugh. From some people the question would have been malicious. In that company and from Hermione Street it was entirely – almost entirely – without sting. It was as if he were being asked whether he would prefer a blue party hat or a red one. Yet at the same time, it was a serious question. Finally he looked back straight into her direct blue gaze.

"I don't know. Perhaps I am a very late developer."

"Perhaps nobody has completed your education," she said.

With a little movement of her outstretched finger tips she touched the two pips on his shoulder. Her arm on the chair back between them was pale and shapely. It was the arm of an odalisque, or a Venus or a Bathsheba; a very naked arm, anyway, and beckoning.

Dorian and a few of the cast went on to a party of their own. The rest of us went on to wherever – I really can't remember – and we danced. Hermione led Hugh in the direction of the music and kept him there.

When, for form's sake, Hermione danced with somebody else, Hugh found me in a corner by the bar.

"What do I do, Verdon?"

"Ah. You are your old self again, Hugh."

I immediately regretted the sarcasm, but Hugh did not notice it.

"I'm afraid I'm not, Verdon."

"Well, you look healthier than you did, anyway."

"I can't account for it, Verdon, but Hermione has made it quite unequivocally clear that she wants to go to bed with me."

"It may have taken her slightly longer to make it clear to you, Hugh, than to the rest of us. You are not mistaken."

"For God's sake, Verdon!"

"Don't you like her? She is rather vain, but very good fun. And extremely beautiful. Oh, and she doesn't offer this privilege to just anybody. She must have taken to you very strongly."

"But her husband, for God's sake."

"Dorian, you mean?"

"He can't be . . . entirely unaware . . ."

"Of course not. But I doubt if there'll be any question of jealousy arising. Unless of course, you think he's fallen for you as well? I gather they have an agreement when that happens. A kind of mutual self-denying ordinance. They do think the world of each other. I'm sure you understand."

"Do I?"

"Of course."

"Oh. Then let's assume I do."

"It's not such an unusual arrangement as all that, Hugh."

"No. I suppose not."

"Don't you want to go to bed with her?"

"Yes, I do. Very much. But then any man who'd just danced with her the way I have would give you the same answer to the same question. The question is, should I? What does it mean? Why does she want to go to bed with me?"

"I suppose her reasons are just as arbitrary as yours. Dance with her again and discuss it to music."

"I don't want those things, Verdon."

"What things?"

"Whatever people mean by falling in love."

"I'm not sure that's necessarily involved, is it?"

"She said as much."

"Well you probably mean something different from what Hermione means. She enjoys falling in love and she is said to have a quite magical talent for it. I gather that it's one of the most exciting and bewildering things that can happen to a man. Being chosen as an object of adoration by Hermione, I mean. I've certainly seen one or two excited and bewildered men in her company."

"Well, you're not about to see another. Make my apologies. Put it down to the hepatitis."

"Shall I call you tomorrow?"

"Please. There are things we have to arrange, after all."

He picked up my glass, drained what little was left in it and in a moment, quietly, had gone.

My job meant having to travel about the country with no obligation to disclose my business and I was, by now, a frequent traveller aboard cadge-as-cadge-can airlines. It made getting to Gwynant easier than it had been before the war, as long as the Anson didn't crash into the side of Snowdon. Several had, and they'd done it in the sort of weather we were flying through. I had felt sick and sad before we took off. I was now sick, sad and frightened, half sitting on, half clinging to the bulky kit bag I had brought along on this trip. The machine was sometimes thrown upwards or downwards so abruptly, and so far, that I could hear and feel the air being sucked in or out of the cabin in noisy, wrenching gasps. Through the window I could see - just - one engine churning its way through the opaque world of black cloud. I called up to the pilot.

"Do you know where we are?"

She pointed casually to an instrument on the panel in front of her.

"Piece of cake," she said.

They really did say things like that. I sat back in my seat and tightened the strap. It passed through my mind that the nonchalance that all aircrew seemed to affect in those days was probably quite genuine. When the odds on dying sooner rather than later had come down as short as they had, the real worry was whether you were going to do it quickly or slowly. Flying into a mountain was probably as quick as you could get, so we were quids in.

The Anson broke cloud over the Menai Straits low enough to rattle the Marquess of Anglesey's windows at Plas Newydd. We followed the coast, a feature that removes all possible doubt from navigation and as I heard the undercarriage cranking down, the prospect of religious conversion receded. I recognised in the distance, pewter bright under a fragment of clear sky between the storms, the wide sands of the estuary by Porth Gwynant. As I watched, and as the Anson's wing swung away, the light moved and the gleam that I knew to be Gwynant vanished again into darkness and distance and black rain.

I scrounged an Austin, but I scrounged one with windscreen wipers that didn't work and it was a long time before I found myself opening the gate at Plas Gwynant.

There was nobody in the lodge now, but there was a pretence of habitation. Curtains had been left at the windows but the dilemma of whether they looked more convincing drawn or open had been resolved by compromise. They were half-drawn.

Stephens heard the Austin on the drive and had opened the door to me before I had reached the steps. He was in shirt-sleeves, but had not omitted the black band of mourning about his right arm.

"I've put you in Mr. Hugh's room, sir, because it was the one room that was always kept aired and ready, but if you'd rather another . . ."

"No. that will suit me very well," I said.

We met in the saloon again. Nothing had changed about the room, and not much among the people, save that Hugh was not there. We had known that we would meet again in this way. It was implicit in everything that we had said and done at that first meeting in that same room, but that fact did not make the heart any lighter. When everyone had taken a seat and Stephens had closed the door, I stood and looked around their faces. They were not expectant, curious or uncertain as they had been on the first occasion. They were composed and resigned, but not, despite the black bands, funereal. They were something more detached than that. It was as if they were waiting in court for some grave sentence to be pronounced on somebody or the other. I am not religious, but I recognise the need for these things.

"It will be right, I think, for us to begin with a prayer."

I could feel that this was approved and together we called upon God, our help in ages past.

After the "Amen" came a hush so deep it was as if the world had fallen mute, which in a way, it had. The rain had stopped.

"I'm sure you'll want to know something about Hugh and how he met his end."

"We have no doubt how he will have met his end," said Tanat. "With very great courage, I am sure."

"That is quite certain," I said. "I meant that I thought you would like to know the circumstances."

Heads nodded and eyes were turned towards me.

"I cannot speak directly about the operation in which Hugh

lost his life, or tell you where it took place. I can tell you that we are going to win this war and before we do we are going to have to put armies ashore on the mainland of Europe. Doing that will be the most hazardous, the most difficult and the most important single effort of the struggle we are in. Knowing what we are going to meet when we reach those beaches will be crucial. Finding out what we shall meet, in the sort of detail that we need, can only be done by going there. It can only be done by men getting onto those beaches at night, by small boats or landed from submarines, to survey the nature and strength of the defences, and sometimes, intentionally or not, to test them. That is the sort of operation for which Hugh volunteered and in which he lost his life."

Tanat was sitting with his gnarled purple hands clenched on the handle of his stick. He pushed his face hard against his knuckles and nodded slightly back and forth.

A little weak sunlight filtered through the tall windows and showed me something brighter in the eyes around the room: the gleam of tears held back. I did not tell them that the operation had been a rehearsal and that Hugh had been drowned when his boat was run down by a submarine. It was a period of confusion in darkness and a bad sea; just the sort of flaw in the plan that rehearsals are meant to uncover. The cost was four men dead in a boat capsized and pulled under the water. Four men for whom no search was made. It was thought they were still on their way to make a landing on the coast of Dorset. It did not matter that it had been a rehearsal, did it? What if it was Dorset? A month later it might have been Dieppe or Deauville.

"There is one great part of our business remaining. The matter of a final resting place for Lord Gwynant. This was left in my hands, as you know, and all the remaining parties with any interest in the matter are now in this room. All the parties with one exception, of course."

They looked at me.

"That is Lord Gwynant. I assume he is still in the house?"

Stephens nodded a butler's assent.

"And his condition has not changed?"

"Changed?" asked Tanat.

"Changed in any way for the worse?" I asked. "I know he could hardly change for the better, but has there been any change for the worse? Has his condition altered in any way that might make for difficulties in moving him?"

"His condition is entirely unaltered," said Tanat. "He has been very well looked after by Mr. Stephens."

There was a very slight note of indignation in Tanat's voice. I nodded apologetically to acknowledge that the question had been superfluous.

"It will be necessary for Lord Gwynant to make an appearance and to be seen at least once more. After that, if I may sketch out his itinerary to you, he will leave Gwynant for London. His plan will be to stay in Mr. Hugh's flat in Westminster where it is expected he will regain his health sufficiently to take occasional walks, especially when his chronic insomnia makes the nights tedious for him. Stephens and Mrs. Bowen will be able to report the frequency of these bouts of insomnia which developed during the latter years at Gwynant. From one of his nocturnal walks he will not return. His disappearance will be reported to the police and added to the list – a very long list – of similar unsolved mysteries on their files."

There was no need for them to know any of the circumstantial details that I had in mind for Lord Gwynant's residence in Westminster. Hugh's flat was in a corner of London that would make the plan easy to carry out with the minimum of subterfuge. It would not be necessary for anyone to see Lord Gwynant in residence, because Hugh's flat was in a corner of London where the policy of the residents was to impinge upon their neighbours as little as possible. His neighbours included Church House and a Catholic convent, inward-looking institutions even before the days of the blackout. It was handy in other ways, too. On Lord Gwynant's final walk he might easily reach the bank of the Thames in a minute, or reach the other side of Westminster Bridge in another five. Or, of course, he might not reach the other side, according to the depth of his depression at the time.

"Are you really going to take his Lordship all the way to London?"

"No, Mrs. Bowen. It is of great importance that there should be no trace of his Lordship to be found in London. This will be easiest to achieve if he is never there."

The next part of my explanation to them was the most difficult. I lived and worked in a world in which it was of vital importance that as many people as possible knew as little as was necessary of the affairs in which they were caught up. I wondered if they realised quite fully that they now lived in the same sort of world. They had, after all, played their parts faithfully and with unfailing discretion. I hoped they would understand that what was required of them now was ignorance. I had to withhold from them any knowledge of the final arrangements for Lord Gwynant's interment.

There is some reason that I should hold it back even now, as the British Government continues to regard certain arrangements of this kind, made during the war years, as matters best kept secret.

You see, the accident that had befallen Hugh was not an unusual occurrence. Training and rehearsal was a great part of our war effort in England in nineteen forty three. The training was often – it had to be – as realistic as possible. That inevitably led to accidents, misfortunes and casualties. A lot of men died as Hugh had died. There were not just a few of them, but thousands. Several entire platoons of American infantry were lost attempting to land on the coast of Pembrokeshire. Canadians, Australians, New Zealanders, as well as our own troops were killed by accident or incompetence in surprisingly large numbers. There were obvious reasons for not publicising these failures. There was an argument for saying that they were not failures but lessons learned; lessons that would lead to eventual successes and the saving of thousands of lives and the shortening of the war.

Still, if they were not failures, they were at least embarassments. No one wanted to tell the folks back in America that they had sent their boys to be drowned or butchered or blown up by mines in the wrong place while trying to liberate Milford Haven. Bodies nowadays are flown home from the furthest zone of war. In those days that was impossible. Men were buried not very far from where they fell. If they fell somewhere embarassingly short of the battlefield itself, they were buried with some honour but little ceremony in plots not conspicuously marked. Somebody was given the job of arranging these discreet funerals. Proper channels were set up for the conduct of the business. My own department sometimes had need to use the services of this department. If you wonder why so much land requisitioned in the war has been retained, even now, by the Ministry of Defence you may reflect that there are in England war graves with no crosses and no memorials to mark them. Their location is reverently marked on maps in the possession of the appropriate department. It is thought best that they should lie undisturbed and unknown. It has been decided that it would not best serve the memory of these gallant but, unfortunately, squandered men that their remains should be turned up by farmers digging drainage or contractors misled into thinking they were building on undisturbed ground.

I had made the necessary arrangements for Lord Gwynant to lie in one of these noble plots. My department was one that, of necessity, called on these arrangements from time to time. It was mainly a matter of knowing who to telephone, though there was a form to be completed. I think I entered Humphrey Vaughan under the category of Irregular Civilian Casualty, a heading which, I'm afraid, covered a multitude of misdemeanours in the treatment of aliens and suspected spies. I think I may also have described him as a British Empire Citizen. I hope so.

It was now necessary to offer the world a last glimpse of Humphrey Vaughan. The advantage of the Daimler was that it was high and capacious and its doors were large. It had required very little contrivance to make it accomodate a passenger in a wheelchair. Two ramps, stowed on the running boards, could be inclined from little brackets so that embarking and disembarking was an easy job. A passenger seated in a wheelchair rode somewhat higher than he would have done on the ordinary seat and the chauffeur was obliged to drive with special care so that the chair did not move dangerously about the compartment. All this conferred a certain majesty on the progress of car and passenger as Jarman drove down the narrow lane from the Plas to Porth Gwynant as the glow of daylight was fading over the sea. Light still gleamed on the peaks of mountains in the east, but night was climbing the slopes.

The Daimler, of course, was not frugal with petrol, but as Lord Gwynant's journeys in it were very infrequent, it had not been difficult to hoard up enough coupons to enable him to motor to Crewe to catch a London train.

His route was to take him by Coed y Bwlch, where Tanat and Emyr waited with the garment that I had provided and that had been in my kit aboard the Anson. I call it a garment, though bag would be more honest. Irregular Casualties were not buried in wooden coffins. They were buried in stout naval canvas. When Tanat and Emyr had prepared his Lordship for his final journey, a detail that involved some re-arrangement of his posture, the Daimler was to continue its journey to Crewe. Except, of course, that it would pass by a certain gate some miles down the road from Coed y Bwlch, and at the edge of the field by that gate I was waiting in a Bedford with a Sergeant of the Pioneer Corps for company. We had parked where we could keep an eye on the road where it crossed a shoulder of the hill a quarter mile away.

The Sergeant was surprisingly good company. The Pioneer Corps' prime function, as the Sergeant put it to me, was 'shifting muck' and the Pioneers were not thought of as providing intellectually stimulating company. On that score, by reputation, the Pioneers came about equal with a regiment of the Cavalry. That is assuming, of course, that you cheat up the intellectual credentials of the cavalry by including the horses. All the same, we whiled away the time playing cribbage in the Bedford's cab and the Sergeant gave me his opinions on the conduct of the war. It was as sound a commentary as I have heard, then or since. His summary was succinct and hard to argue with. "It's one fucking fuck up after another. And when they've done, they'll only go and fuck it up again." It was the prescience that I thought impressive.

The Sergeant had just unfolded a hand that put him in a winning position and was moving the half-burnt match along the board when I saw what I hoped were the Daimler's shrouded lights moving over the shoulder of the hill.

"Your game."

I gave him the half-crown and he spun it expertly into the air with a flick of his thumb, caught it and made it disappear into his pocket with a magician's flourish.

"Ta, very much. Give you another game whenever you like."

I climbed down from the cab, taking the red shaded torch with me. Pinning the gate back with a stone, I picked my way as carefully as I could around the muddied patch and into the road.

A few moments later I was in no doubt. It was the Daimler. Nothing else could have been so bulky against the sky and making so lazy a noise. I flicked the red shade off the torch and signalled the turn through the gate into the field.

It seemed I was mistaken. The car came on steadily down the lane, with no sign of stopping. I stepped out and held the torch up straight in front of me where there was no possibility of the driver's failing to see it.

And then I knew that it was the Daimler. The light of my torch fell on Jarman at the wheel. Apart from pulling over the road to miss me, he did not acknowledge me at all. As the car passed, the light of my torch brushed the figure in the back. Lord Gwynant was sitting upright and leaning a little forward. He jolted in his seat as he went by. The Daimler had passed me and was gone into the darkness. Perhaps it was the movement and the shadow. Or perhaps since Tanat had done his work a certain dessication had changed the set of the features. I would not call it a laugh, or even a smile, but Lord Gwynant's expression impressed itself on me in that brief glimpse by a pallid light. The little sharp glint of his teeth put it somewhere between a laugh and a sneer. Or it might have been the frozen beginning of a scream.

I stood in the darkness and switched off the torch.

"Wrong lot?" asked the sergeant.

"No. Right lot," I said.

"'Nother fuck up."

"Yes. It seems so."

"Drive after 'em?"

I thought for a few moments, but not many.

"No."

I had the sergeant drop me at Tanat's cottage. There was nobody at home but the door was unlocked, as such doors always were in those days. I let myself in, lit a lamp and took a seat beside a fire whose coals were not quite dead.

I had not much more than an hour to wait before I heard their boots on the lane, and heard them pause, seeing the lamplight. I imagine that in the pause they shared a certain hesitation about who was to enter and face me first. It was Emyr, but all he did was nod to me before hanging his hat behind the door. He walked over to the fire and poked at it. The last of the ashy coals fell through the bars with a few drooping sparks. All the same he continued to stare at the hearth, as if waiting for the fire to blaze up.

Tanat hung his hat.

"Would you care for a bottle of beer, Mr. James?" He said and stepped out into the scullery.

"We just come back from the house," said Emyr. "Mr. Stephens was going to tell you all about it."

"As I'm here, perhaps you would be kind enough to tell me now."

I let my eye fall on the bag of stout naval canvas that lay

rolled on the floor beneath the table. The cat was just then moving in a circle on the top of it, making a depression into which it settled. Emyr glanced at it and then back to the poker in his hand.

"Dad best, I think."

Tanat came back in from the scullery with two bottles of beer. The bottles were old and dusty and their stoppers were clenched with rusty wire. He wiped each with his shirt sleeve and stood them on the table.

"Emyr, fetch a mug, boy. A glass for Mr. James. Be sure it is clean."

"Where did Jarman go with Lord Gwynant?"

"A quiet place, Mr. James."

"Why? Why did you not do as we agreed?"

"There was a meeting after."

"It was agreed by everybody," said Emyr, coming back from the scullery with two mugs and a glass. The glass had the name of a public house etched on it and when he gave it to me I took out my handkerchief and began to wipe it.

"I'm sorry if it is not clean," said Emyr.

"I'm just giving it a polish, Emyr. I think this is slightly special beer."

"We shall see if it has been keeping," said Tanat, but his old hands were defeated by the rusty wire. He handed the job to Emyr, who took out his knife and prised the wire from the neck of each bottle.

The beer had been keeping very well. As it was more than fifty years old, it was miraculous that it was drinkable at all but it was better than drinkable. It was dark and still, dense and rich to the taste.

We looked at each other and that was enough. There was no need for comment.

"What does that mean, Mr. James? I'm sure you will know."

Tanat pointed to the embossed medallion on the bottle.

"Gaudeamus? It means 'let us rejoice,' Tanat."

He turned the bottle round as if to make sure that the words were what they always had been.

"Perhaps it is not appropriate. We shall not rejoice, no. But we prefer things as they have been, Mr. James." Emyr nodded.

"Everybody is agreed. We prefer things as they have been."

I took a sip of the strange beer. It was hard to know where to begin to explain to them the impossibility of their position.

"Now that Mr. Hugh is no longer here, who is to conduct the affairs of the estate? Every year there are a hundred things to do, business to be attended to. Hugh's cousin must inherit. Lord Gwynant must be properly and decently buried."

"Mr. Hugh's cousin is a boy of military age."

"He is in the Navy, I think. Yes."

They looked at me as if a look said all they wished.

"The problem of death duties is different now," I said. "Mr. Hugh left all of his interest in the estate in a trust."

"And you are trustee, Mr. James," said Emyr.

"Surely there is the answer to the question you ask," said Tanat.

"I would naturally step aside when Hugh's cousin David inherits. It is essential that that should happen."

"He will inherit if he survives."

"Tanat. Lord Gwynant must be laid to rest and the duty paid. And that's all there is to it."

Tanat drank his beer very slowly from the mug. He drank it with great attention.

"We prefer things as they have been."

I got back to London in need of distraction. Diana was out of town but Hermione was usually 'at home' on certain afternoons if she was not in rehearsal. It was one of those afternoons and I called, slightly earlier than was entirely polite.

She called a greeting from the drawing room as I climbed the stairs. "Her voice always tinkles," said one of the critics, "but sometimes it tinkles like a silver spoon on china and sometimes like an entire crystal chandelier crashing to the floor."'

That afternoon it was a strangely muffled tinkling.

She was sitting on a straight-backed chair close to the window as if she were sitting for a portrait. A view over the tops of trees and out to the Park beyond was the background. A young woman in overalls, whom I thought at first to be a hairdresser was bending attentively over her.

"You mayn't kiss me I'm afraid. Not just yet. Find yourself something to drink. This will not quite take forever."

She rolled her eyes at the young woman, who took no notice but walked around to the other side of Hermione, opened up an instrument like a pair of forceps and then closed its tips gently on her head. One tip went on her occiput and one about the bridge of her nose.

The young woman made a note on a pad that lay beside her, then took up another position and closed the calipers again on Hermione's head.

"It's nothing to do with phrenology, darling, I promise. I'm being measured for Madame Tussaud's. Are you impressed?"